TIME OUT:
DETROIT SLIM

A Double Book Experience by
Geavonnie Frazier

Q-Boro Books

WWW.QBOROBOOKS.COM

An Urban Entertainment Company

Published by Q-Boro Books
Copyright © 2006 by Geavonnie Frazier

ISBN 1-933967-07-2
First Printing September 2006

10 9 8 7 6 5 4 3 2 1

Cover Copyright © 2006 by Q-BORO BOOKS all rights reserved
Cover Layout & Design – Candace K. Cottrell
Photo by Ted Mebane
Editors – Melissa Forbes, Candace K. Cottrell

Q-BORO BOOKS
Jamaica, Queens NY 11431
WWW.QBOROBOOKS.COM

Dedication

This book is dedicated to my daughter Kailah
and to my beloved sisters
Etta Jean Frazier 1960- 1981 &
Maryann Frazier 1957-2001

TIME OUT

By

Geavonnie Frazier

If you don't stand for something,
you will fall for anything

PROLOGUE

The sound of sobbing came through the receiver.

"They got me, playa."

The sniffling had muffled the sound of the spinning barrel of the .38 special he had palmed in his hand.

"Who got you?"

"The bitches. They got me, nigga. After all the bullshit I ran on these hoes, it finally came home to rest," he said as if he knew that one day it was going to happen.

"You're talking crazy now. Why don't you come over so we can talk?"

"I got that bitch real good for you. She let me hit it raw, my nigga. So now she has what she deserves, but I'm not going to succumb. I control my own destiny."

"I hope you ain't talking about killing yourself. You got me nervous."

"Don't you know that we're already in hell and death just puts us in the final line of judgment? Ain't no need for you to try to be no hero, dawg. By the time you do find me, it'll be too late. I just called to let you know that I love you and I'm sorry."

The man dropped his cell phone and placed the loaded .38 special into his mouth. He took a slow breath and then pulled trigger, blowing his brains out of his skull and onto the driver and passenger windows of his 2006 Maybach 57 S.

CHAPTER ONE

Saturday night is club night in downtown Detroit, better known as Motown or The Motor City. Detroit is the home of gator shoes, the big three automakers, the movers and the shakers, the original players, and the two-dollar car wash. Daunte and his boy, Antonio, a.k.a. Pretty Tony, were popping bottles of champagne at one of the hottest nightspots in the city. Detroit is a city of haute couture, so the club was packed with people dressed up like they were getting ready to walk down a runway. The guys were dressed in tailored Armani and Versace suits. The ladies were styling in the latest Prada and Gucci apparel. You could see fellas walking around the bar with their Dobbs tilted to the side, trying to get their mack on with every woman who came up to get a drink.

Tonight was live. Daunte was checking out a couple of chickenheads he wanted to holla at. He decided to make his move on a little sexy chocolate mami who was wearing a white strapless dress that showed off her complexion and strappy silver heels. She stood near the DJ's booth conversing with her taller female companion who was decked out in a slinky green halter dress with matching stilettos.

Lisa was in the middle of her conversation with Tosha when Daunte approached. He overheard her talking about how some nigga paid her rent and how the nigga thought he was going to get some pussy for the deed. The two ladies laughed at the notion as Daunte walked up and joined them in their laughter. Lisa rolled her eyes as he made his uninvited presence known.

"Excuse you," Lisa said, feeling perturbed.

"Calm down. I just came over to offer you a drink," Daunte replied.

"OK, I'll take two apple martinis," she said as she returned to her conversation with Tosha, treating Daunte as if he were a server for the club.

Daunte turned to her friend and asked if she would like anything from the bar. Lisa was impressed with his generosity. After taking their orders, he returned juggling the three drinks.

"Aw, that was sweet," Tosha stated.

"Yeah, that was nice," Lisa agreed.

Lisa downed the two drinks and grabbed Daunte by the hand, leading him through the crowd of drunks and ass-grabbers. Once they finally reached the dance floor, she ostentatiously started shaking and popping her ass all over the place. The guys who played pool nearby even stopped their game to watch. Daunte congratulated himself for picking out a real freak. He just stood there as she grinded on his hardening love joy. Her ass was so big that when she gyrated it bumped him back every time he tried to dance with her.

After a couple of songs passed, the dance floor emptied to make way for the jitt competition. Jitt is to Detroit what the Harlem Shake is to New York and the Crip Walk is to Cali. Lisa and Daunte briefly watched the majestic footwork before heading back to find Tosha. They met up with Tosha and were discussing plans for the night when Daunte was shoved by a big, ugly-ass muthafucka. The beast stood almost seven feet from the ground and looked as if he weighed as much as a whale.

"Damn, nigga, you better watch where the fuck you goin'!" Daunte said.

The killer giant turned around, casting his shadow as it swallowed the dim light that shined between them.

"Mr. Burnt Out Pete!" Daunte said, recognizing his childhood friend.

The two females had made their escape to the other side of the club when they turned around and witnessed the two men laughing and talking. Vexed, Tosha and Lisa returned after pushing off about thirty niggas. They finally made it back to Daunte, who didn't acknowledge them until Lisa finally spoke.

"Yo, we thought it was about to be some shit," Lisa said, trying to laugh off her embarrassment. Daunte could care less about them leaving. He didn't expect those hoes to stick around if shit went down anyway.

Burnt Out Pete was Daunte's boy since sixth grade, and he had met Antonio the year after that . Daunte and Pete met at a Junior League baseball game on West 7 Mile Road near Greenfield. Pete was trying to impress Daunte and the rest of the kids by telling jokes about how tight the umpire's pants were fitting. After that failed to get the children's attention, Pete resorted to lighting a joint. When he saw their look of amazement, he began what he called *Puff the Magic Dragon*, which was a very big mistake. One of the kids who Pete swore he was so revered by ran back to tell his dad, who just happened to be an off-duty narcotics officer for the Detroit Police Department.

Two white uniformed officers arrived shortly after and placed the six-foot sixth grader into handcuffs. The officers' attitudes were temperate until they put Pete in the squad car. That's when Pete said he became all types of ugly, black-ass niggers and porch monkeys. When Pete decided to inform them that their mothers had on occasion enjoyed his big, black, porch monkey dick, they retorted by beating the already dark-skinned brother to a serious blackish blue.

Burnt Out Pete got his nickname for a variety of reasons. One was that he smoked entirely too much weed, but Pretty Tony believed they called him that because it looked like his mama tried to bake his ass in the oven right after he was born.

"I see you still got the hoes," Pete said at the arrival of the ladies.

"Who your ugly ass calling a ho?" Lisa demanded to know.

Daunte knew the word *bitch* was bound to come out of Pete's mouth, so he quickly interrupted.

"Dog, hold up! Let me holla at you for a minute." Daunte and Pete spoke off to the side and he explained to Pete how he needed to chill because he was about to fuck up his pussy for the night.

"My bad, dog, I'm fucked up right about now."

"That's cool, but let me wrap this shit up and I'll holla' at you in a second."

Pete turned and gave Lisa a daunting look, but it flew right over her head. Daunte and Pete gave each other dap and then Pete pushed his way through the crowd.

"That nigga was tripping!" Lisa said long after Pete had made it to the other side of the club.

"So where are we going for breakfast?" Daunte asked in a deep and sexy tone, trying to throw her off the subject by licking his lips.

Lisa watched as his tongue slide back into his mouth, wishing she could follow.

"It don't matter as long as we eat," Lisa said as Tosha agreed.

Pretty Tony walked up to the trio and immediately Tosha was all in his face before Daunte had a chance to introduce him.

"Tosha, Lisa, this is my man, Pretty Tony."

"Nice to meet you, ladies." Pretty Tony smiled, revealing his straight pearly whites before kissing their hands.

Tosha kept staring at him with an inane smile, which made her look like a groupie. He was used to this kind of behavior from women. They reacted that way around him all the time. Tosha was very beautiful with her smooth, caramel skin and hazel eyes, and her body was the shape of an hourglass. Pretty Tony didn't have any complaints. They made plans to meet out front in about half an hour to go get breakfast. The ladies departed as Daunte and Antonio walked over to the bar. Daunte ordered three shots of 1800 and Antonio grabbed himself an Incredible Hulk.

"You got some fine ones tonight!" Antonio said right before Burnt Out Pete strolled his big ass between the two with a huge smile on his face.

Pete was wearing blue jeans, a hoodie, and a pair of Air Force Ones. That shit was cool to wear at *Dress to Sweat,* but this was *Soul Night,* Detroit's mini player's ball. This was where the players and pimpettes came out styling with their gators and furs. *Soul Night* had been losing its class over the last couple of years by letting in anybody, wearing whatever.

"What up, pretty ass niggas? Where the hoes at?" Pete asked, excited like a little-ass boy.

"Mr. Burnt Out Pete! Where the weed at?" Antonio asked.

When it came to weed, Pete kept the funk. Pete put his weed in red bags to signify he had that fire.

"What you need? A pound? An ounce? Whatever you want, I got it."

"What you got on you now?" Pretty Tony asked.

"I just got a couple of quarter bags."

Just as Pete reached to show him the bags, a foxy, brown-skinned, five foot five young lady walked directly up to Daunte, interrupting their conversation.

"Is your name Daunte?"

"Who wants to know?" Daunte crossed his arms.

"Me, silly. I met you at the Candy Bar a few months ago. You were supposed to take me out to breakfast at the casino, but your ass was nowhere to be found when they closed down the club." The woman crossed her arms and nodded her head for effect.

Daunte could not recall. To make plans with a chick for breakfast after the club was a ritual. She was fine as hell, and he couldn't understand why he would have passed up an opportunity to try to take her back to his place.

"Oh yeah, I remember now. I tried to find you before I left, but I couldn't."

"Negro, please, I know you probably left with some little freak and got you some booty that night."

Pete derided Daunte for getting caught up.

"Naw, I don't know what you're talking about. Fuck that, what's up wit tonight? I'll make it up to you."

"Where are you talking about going?" she asked, toning her voice down a bit.

"We can go back to my crib and I'll make you some homemade breakfast."

She paused for a moment before answering. "That's cool. But first, what's my name, since you want to take me home for breakfast and shit?"

Before he could even muster a lie, she decided to let him off the hook by telling him that her name was Crystal.

"I'll be outside in ten minutes, and if you're not out there, then there won't be a next time," Crystal said as she brushed her breast up against him and walked off.

"It's train time, nigga. She a straight up freak," Burnt Out Pete declared.

Pretty Tony and Daunte looked at each other, knowing Pete was not going to be part of any of their plans for tonight. Pete was infamous for messing up shit. He once fucked up an Ecstasy orgy with ten women who Daunte lined up for the three of them. He was too irascible. He would start a shouting match with a female if she acted as though she wasn't interested. That's why Pete was *not* allowed to take part in their outings.

"Damn, what about Lisa?" Daunte spoke his thoughts out loud.

He had to make a decision. Lisa was thick as hell, but Crystal was a dime piece. He decided he would go out with Crystal, and Antonio would have to manage the other two women, which he didn't mind doing at all. Pete pointed at some chick who walked right past him without speaking or acknowledging that he even existed.

"Yo, you see that freak right there? I had to tell that hoodrat to stop calling me, dawg. She was blowing up my two-way pager like a mutherfucka, nigga. I mean, like every day!" Pete bragged.

Daunte and Antonio didn't really pay any attention to Pete's boasting, because it always seemed as if he was trying too hard to impress them by talking about how many hoes he supposedly had jocking him. After Pete's digression, Daunte asked him for the two quarters that he had left. They made the drug transaction and Daunte tossed Antonio a bag and said "peace" before he headed for coat check.

Lisa and Tosha were contemplating leaving when Antonio walked up to them, grinning like the devil. He explained that Daunte had an emergency and would be meeting up with them at the restaurant. Lisa was skeptical of the idea, but still agreed to go. The plan was to follow Antonio to the restaurant and Daunte would arrive by the time they ordered.

Pete stood in the shadows, watching as his so-called boys left him out to dry.

"Karma's a bitch, mothafuckas," he mumbled.

CHAPTER TWO

Crystal stood shivering in front of the club, staring at the time on her cell phone. She thought to herself that Daunte's ass had one minute left before she was out. The doors swung open with loud music and chatter escaping from the club as a horde of people exited. Crystal's eyes searched and located Daunte trying to make his way out of the small group of people who were leaving. She stared at the fine man, admiring his sexy, full lips. She wondered how soft his lips might feel against hers or maybe even against her hardening nipples. She couldn't understand why she was thinking that way. She had never considered herself to be a freak, but now she was going home for "breakfast" with a guy she barely knew.

Crystal had lived a very sheltered life. When she was younger, her father forced her to go to an all-girls school. Her dad was a very strict man. He was a retired and bitter general from the U.S. Marines. He hated and scared away every guy she tried to date, except for David Alan. David Alan was the son of one of her father's platoon buddies who had saved his life back in Vietnam. Crystal's father believed that David was the perfect man for her to marry, and he was even following in his father's footsteps by joining the Marines after he graduated from high school.

David was short, dark, and far as hell from handsome. David stayed next door, and every day he and her father would bug her about being his girl, until one day she finally gave in. At the age of fourteen, she would have never guessed that she would be with the same lame guy for so long. Crystal eventually fell in love with David, and soon after he took her virginity. But David quickly turned into a mirror image of her dad. At times he was very cruel and controlling.

It was little things that began to bother her about David. For instance, he would go months without a haircut and he hated to iron or even take his clothes to the dry cleaners. David really turned her off when he would leave out the house wearing wrinkled-ass clothes. For a long time, she believed he couldn't be from Detroit because he had no sense of style. She recalled the day she bought him a gabardine suit for his birthday. He wore it for homecoming with a pair of gray Rockports and sweat socks. That was another thing that turned her off. Especially when she saw her friends out with their boyfriends and dates dressed nicely together.

She still tried to have a good time, but he even refused to dance with her. So they sat all night with the white of his tube socks beaming from underneath the eight-hundred-dollar money-green suit that she had wasted on him. She laughed to herself for being so stupid to spend that much money on his ass in the first place.

Eventually Crystal ended her relationship with David, but he didn't take it well at all. He began stalking her, peeking in her window, and constantly calling her at all times of the night. Her father actually became indignant even after she told him the reasons why she broke up with the psycho. Finally the time came for David to leave for boot camp. The night he left, Crystal and her girlfriends celebrated. For once in her life, she was going to be free.

Crystal wanted to see what else was out there, but she didn't find much—until tonight when she saw Daunte again. She had watched Daunte go around the club, smiling and collecting number after number. She wanted to laugh at the brother because he thought he was so smooth. She found herself mesmerized with him, even now as he approached. His Casanova charms were inexorable. Could it be those seductive eyes that seemed to undress her with each word he spoke? That really had turned her on. It was normally the ugly muthafuckas who gave her that much attention. She always believed the cute ones were too intimidated to try something like that on her. As Daunte made his way out of the crowd, Crystal noticed him smiling at her, revealing two of the prettiest dimples. His face was shaped almost like a pear because of his strong, high cheekbones. To her, he was definitely a fine brother. He was clean-shaven with his hair corn-rowed to the back. He had thick black eyebrows that floated over his surreptitious dark brown eyes. His skin was a smooth cocoa butter complexion and his body had a slim build with a muscular tone. His only shortcoming was that she knew he smoked weed. But Crystal was tired of dating the huge, bodybuilder types like David. Daunte was a pretty boy who seemed to attract a lot of females. She couldn't ever recall having to worry about female competition when it came to David.

"You OK?" Daunte asked, looking at her suspiciously and hoping she wasn't a psycho or something.

"Yeah, I'm cool." Crystal looked at him from head to toe.

Daunte smelled good and was dressed nicely too. He wore a cream and white Versace suit with the matching gators and a full-length white mink. Daunte handed the valet his ticket to bring around his Navigator. Crystal got a ride with her girls to the club, so he didn't have to escort her to her car. Daunte tipped the attendant and opened the door for Crystal to get in. Crystal buckled up and began to laugh to herself again as Daunte made his way into the driver's seat.

"I was just thinking about something. Don't pay me any attention," Crystal said, still smiling.

"OK," Daunte replied as he began to feel dubious about taking her back to his place.

CHAPTER THREE

"Where is this nigga goin'? We've been following his ass for the last twenty minutes."

"Shut up, girl. You always complaining," Tosha replied and then pointed out that there was a pancake house coming up.

They followed Antonio into the half-empty parking lot. Antonio turned his car around so his window was facing the driver's.

"Look, its only three cars here. I ain't feeling this. Follow me back to my crib and I'll make some bacon and waffles or something."

Lisa complained to Tosha that she wanted to go home and call it a night. Going back to his place to her was some bullshit.

"Tony, follow me for a minute, I gotta take Lisa home," Tosha said, causing a shocked reaction from Lisa.

What the fuck is Tosha thinking? Lisa thought to herself. She knew that her sleep would have to wait because she was not going to let her girl go to this nigga's place alone.

"Girl, I'm straight. I can ride. I was a little tired at first, but I'm up now."

"All right, Tony, I guess I'm ready to follow you," Tosha said while giving Tony an apologetic look.

Antonio wasn't upset that Lisa was coming. He was totally indifferent about the situation. He had prevailed before in worse situations of cock blocking.

They arrived at Pretty Tony's opulent apartment. As soon as they walked in, the custom silk sectional sofa that was combined with stone and wood furnishings greeted them and offered a comfortable retreat to watch the sunrise. The front room featured butted glass window walls that jutted out toward the Detroit River like the bow of a ship.

Tony let the ladies go on a self-guided tour while he made breakfast. Lisa was surprised by his taste. She especially enjoyed his collection of African masks displayed on floating shelves in the study. His apartment was decorated with a creative intellect. Lisa felt herself being turned on by the light-skinned, long-and-curly-haired playboy. Antonio was made up of a variety of ethnicities and races. His dad was black and his mom was Greek, Italian, and Indian. He was short with a muscular build, and he wore a full, dark beard. The only thing that held Lisa back from trying to fuck him right then was the fact that her girl had her eyes on him first.

By the time they finished viewing his apartment, stopping in each room and staring at the décor, and discussing it as if they were in an art museum, Antonio had made scrambled eggs, waffles, bacon, and hash browns. Lisa noticed how there wasn't any mention of Daunte since they had arrived, but she didn't care at all because she was enjoying Antonio's company anyway.

"I like the piranha bedroom set that you have in the master bedroom. I wouldn't mind falling asleep on that," Lisa said to Tony as he emptied a bag of weed onto the kitchen counter.

Tosha had noticed that Lisa was starting to become a little too flirtatious toward Tony and decided to disparage her for her comments.

"Oh you mean that *Prada* bedroom set? Girl, that sho' was cute." Tosha laughed sarcastically.

Lisa snapped her head back and gave Tosha a sour look as if she had just bitten into a lemon. A catfight was about to begin, but was quickly put on hold when Tony lit up and passed them the bong. Lisa and Tosha smoked and got so high that they forgot about the food, the bickering, and the fact they weren't bisexual.

Tony motioned for the women to follow him to the living room. He turned on some soft music and reclined on the chaise lounge, where he began ordering them around.

"Lisa, baby, I want you to slowly undress ya girl."

Lisa looked to Tosha, and then to Tony with glazed eyes as a giggle escaped from her full lips. She looked directly into Tosha's eyes as her hands slowly moved from her own neck to Tosha's. She turned Tosha around, lifted Tosha's golden, curly hair, and untied the green halter straps. The fabric of the dress was so slinky that it seemed to immediately glide off Tosha's body, where it formed a pool at her feet.

With Tosha's bare caramel back and gold rhinestone thong staring him in the face, another idea come to Tony.

"Tosha, bend over and touch your toes. I wanna see that pussy smile at me."

As Tosha bent at the waist and began swaying her ass back and forth, Lisa removed her own dress and stood there staring at Tosha's display. Getting mad turned on from the effects of the weed, the moans coming from Tony as he softly stroked himself, and Tosha's bare pussy staring her in the face, Lisa slid her fingers inside her own panties, fingering the wetness that now lingered there.

"Touch her," Tony ordered Lisa.

A bit bashful, but too hot and bothered to care, Lisa dropped to her knees, slid Tosha's thong to the side, and slowly stoked her from front to back. She could smell the sweetness emanating from Tosha's honey pot and her mouth began to water.

A soft moan escaped Tosha's lips as she felt Lisa's tongue exploring her. She turned around and positioned herself on the soft rug that covered the floor. Lisa leaned down to taste her friend again and felt Tony's warmth behind her.

Tony smacked Lisa's ass and moved his hands across her bare bottom. He reached his hand around and stroked her clit while she made a feast of Tosha. A low moan escaped Lisa's lips and transferred the vibration to Tosha's experience.

Lisa gasped when Tony entered her, and this prompted her to speed up the pace with Tosha. While she rhythmically flicked her girl's clit with her tongue, she inserted two fingers into Tosha's wet cave.

"Oh, shit. Oh, shit. I'm coooomiiinnng," Tosha screamed.

This made Tony shift into straight-up fucking, and he started pounding into Lisa's tightness. When he was done, they all switched positions and went for round two. After Tony sexed both of them, he watched the two women eat each other out as he lay back and enjoyed the show.

CHAPTER FOUR

Daunte and Crystal were driving northbound on the Southfield Freeway, heading toward Daunte's place.

"You better know how to cook, since you're inviting me over to your crib for breakfast," Crystal said, smiling and waiting for Daunte's response.

"You ain't got to worry about that, love. I'm a certified cook. You name it, I can flame it."

Crystal chuckled at his boasting and began to sing along with Alicia Keys's "A Woman's Worth" while it played from the CD changer. Something about tonight felt nice to her. She was finally out with what she hoped was a real man. He was funny, but still charming. She admired his laid-back approach. He was definitely smooth. He spoke with a lion's confidence, yet his personality showed no signs of conceit.

To Crystal, she was on a date, although she was pretty sure that he thought of it as just another booty call after the club. She wasn't cool with that title, but she wanted to have sex, too. It'd been eleven months of abstinence, but tonight that was about to change.

This lucky brother is getting some tonight, she thought, arousing herself.

Yeah, tonight she would finally let out all her sexual frustrations and there would be no holding back.

As long as he doesn't say anything stupid to fuck it up, she concluded to herself as they pulled into the driveway of his Rosedale Park home.

Once inside, Daunte made himself some pancakes, sausage, bacon, ham, eggs, and grits. For her, he made pancakes and a veggie omelet because she didn't like pork. After breakfast, he turned the lights down and lit about a dozen candles. He moved gracefully across the room, lighting the logs that nestled between the bricks of the chimney.

"Let's make a toast," Daunte said while pouring two glasses of champagne and passing one to Crystal.

"What are we toasting to?" Crystal asked while sipping the spilled bubbly that ran from her glass.

"To a new and hopefully special beginning," he said.

They toasted and drank the whole bottle of Cristal, along with about six shots of Patron. Daunte offered Crystal to hit the blunt that he had just rolled, but she refused. She told him that she didn't smoke and thought that smoking was very unattractive. Daunte didn't mind putting the blunt away. He wasn't a heavy smoker anyway. He only smoked sometimes on the weekend, when he didn't have important business to take care of. Besides all that, the Patron with the Cristal chaser had given them a nice buzz.

Daunte asked Crystal to follow him, leading her down the hall and up a few stairs to the den. He popped open another bottle of champagne after they sat down on the bearskin rug that lay collapsed in front of another fireplace. With the remote control, Daunte turned on the CD player, skipped to disc six, and played track number two on Jaheim's CD.

They stared into each other's eyes for a moment before they kissed. It was passionate and intense, and Crystal felt herself shivering from the tongue play. Daunte laid her back. She closed her eyes as she felt her top come off in one move. She was almost naked in a minute's time.

She opened her eyes to see his tongue moving in motion to taste the whipped cream he was squeezing onto her breasts. He began to lick around her nipples slowly before sucking off the melting cream. His head went downward as he kissed her stomach and licked the inside of her navel. He moved his face down further to her thighs and licked her outer lips, teasing her until she moaned. Daunte covered her lower region with the whipped cream, licking and sucking until she moaned in ecstasy. Her legs jerked from the orgasm. He brought himself up and kissed her, placing his penis inside her as her legs greeted him with a hug. They moved slowly at first, in perfect rhythm with the music. But when Crystal said, "Fuck me, Daunte," it sped up to a feverish rhythm. Daunte flipped her over and hit it from the back while Crystal moaned and stroked her swollen clit. Almost simultaneously, they exploded in pleasure.

CHAPTER FIVE

At seven o'clock the next morning Antonio's phone rang about three times before he reluctantly reached over to answer it.

"Hello?" Antonio answered, sounding half sleep.

"Nigga, I ain't drinking no more!" Daunte shouted angrily.

"What happened?" Antonio asked as he sat up.

"Dog, I fucked homegirl from last night without a muthafuckin' rubber. I tried to play it off, so I asked her why she let me hit without a rubber."

"What?" Antonio asked as he began laughing.

Daunte overheard a female's voice in the background asking Antonio who was on the phone.

"Bitch, it ain't none of your muthafuckin' business who I'm on the phone with!" Antonio screamed to his overnight guest.

"Oh hell naw, I'm out of here!" Lisa said as she hopped out the bed, butt ass naked, grabbing for her things.

Antonio looked over to Tosha, who stayed behind in the bed. He told her to take her friend home and he would call her later. Antonio waited until the women got dressed and made their way out of his apartment before he continued his conversation. Daunte started to hang up, but curiosity kept him on the line to find out what had just taken place.

"You fucked both of them last night?" Daunte asked, almost sure he already knew the answer.

"And you know this, man!" Antonio replied as the men began to laugh.

Antonio asked him to continue with his story about his late night rendezvous.

"Oh yeah, so she said to me, 'It's a little too late to be asking that now, don't you think?' So I asked her how many guys she had sex with without wearing a rubber. She told me that she had only been with two people without protection: her first and some dude that she met off the damn Internet!" Daunte screamed into the phone.

"Yeah right, you know she been with more than that. They always say, 'I can count on one hand how many I've been with' or 'You're the first that I have had sex with in a long time,'" Antonio advised while laughing at Daunte's frustration.

Daunte ignored him and proceeded to tell him the rest of the story. He asked Crystal if she had ever been tested and she replied that she hadn't. That stressed him so badly that he lit his blunt. Her complaining about him sparking didn't mean shit to him at that point. He puffed smoke clouds into her face out of the disgust he was feeling. Then, out of nowhere, she began to play with herself, moving the covers off her, and revealing her long, silky legs. She gave him a full show, but he paid her no attention. By the time the blunt was half gone, he was finally taking notice of her masturbation. She opened her eyes and caught him staring in heat. She played on that by taking the blunt from him as she climbed on top of him. She rubbed his penis against her clit and then placed it inside her. She was so wet that he couldn't manage the strength to even think about stopping her.

"Man, that shit felt so good!" Daunte said to Antonio as both men laughed. "But on a serious note, I'm not getting fucked up anymore because I can't afford to keep doing stupid shit like that. Did you use a rubber with those chicks from last night?" Daunte asked Antonio.

"How can you wear a rubber when you're with two women?" Antonio answered.

Easily, dumb mutherfucka, Daunte thought. But how could he judge him when he had also made the same stupid-ass mistake?

CHAPTER SIX

Daunte sat thinking about the direction in which his life was going. He had attended an all-black university in DC, where he had made friends who actually went after their dreams. That was something he rarely saw while growing up in his old neighborhood.

He recalled meeting one of his college buddies by the name of Marcus Fallon during their freshman year when they modeled in the Homecoming Fashion Show. Marcus was six foot two, dark brown, and baldheaded with hazel-brown eyes. Daunte didn't know it at the time, but the eye color was the result of contacts. The two met backstage at the fashion show and Marcus asked Daunte what club he was going to for the after-party. Daunte wasn't going anywhere except back to his dorm room to be with his girlfriend at the time, who didn't like to do much of anything. But that would be the last time he would miss out on partying because of a relationship. He made up for it during his next three years of college.

Marcus and Daunte didn't hang out that first night, but they exchanged numbers and soon became good friends. They were recognized everywhere they went. They were known by almost the whole university. They would go to all the movie premieres on campus, the frat parties, poetry slams, and chill on the yard regularly when they were on a break from class. All those places were also hot spots for them to catch girls. Daunte was the aggressive one. He would holla at any female who looked good, and it didn't matter where they were. He could catch a girl walking in the rain, running late to class, and without an umbrella, and still get her phone number.

Marcus, on the other hand, was shy when it came to talking to women. After being around Daunte so much, he had no choice but to become a little bit more talkative. Women started to think he was weird because Daunte was so outgoing and he was reserved. As a student Marcus did well. He was very intelligent. The one thing that brought him down was something he couldn't learn in any textbook. What he lacked was street knowledge. Marcus loved to be out with thugs in the hard ghetto streets of the Chocolate City. But he didn't grow up in a big city. He grew up in a small, predominately hick town in Wisconsin. He was like Carlton from *The Fresh Prince* with a doo-rag and Timbs.

By his junior year, smoking weed and not going to class had cost Marcus his scholarship. He began working as a busboy in the Adams Morgan area. He no longer liked going to hip hop night at clubs. He wanted to go to rave parties and ride skateboards to campus. Soon after, he began popping cold pills to catch a different high with his new punk rocker friends. Every time Daunte would go by Marcus's sordid apartment, there would be piles of empty beer cans and trash all over the floor. When he saw Marcus, he smelled like he hadn't showered in weeks. Marcus complained that Daunte spent too much time fucking with females, and he believed that Daunte should try other things, like playing basketball or skateboarding.

Daunte's biggest problem was that he was good with women. So women became his extracurricular activity after classes and studying. Other guys might have excelled at sports and other things, but Daunte's talent was more challenging. He was the best at conquering and taming the most confusing creatures on earth—women. Daunte couldn't understand how his friend could go from being a 3.8 student and a fellow playa, to becoming a fiend living in filth. He knew Marcus was a follower, but he didn't expect that he would be traveling down the road that he was going. Once the cold pills no longer gave him the same effect, he went from weed to cocaine, and in his own self-delusions tried to convince Daunte to try it. After that, Daunte decided to put an end to their friendship.

A couple of months passed and Marcus moved to California to live with a white girl he had known for less than three weeks. He found her ad in the singles section of the local paper. It was rumored that she also used coke and often made derogatory jokes about blacks to Marcus. The last thing Daunte heard about his old college pal was that he was doing odd jobs like painting and cutting grass in the Bay Area to support his habit.

CHAPTER SEVEN

Daunte was a substitute teacher for the Wayne County School District. He was covering an English class at Miller Middle School in Detroit for the week. The English teacher, Mr. Johnson, had taken off because of a death in his family. He left the class with an assignment to cut out an article out of the obituary section of the newspaper and explain how they felt when they read it. Daunte's instructions were to take their assignment home and grade the essay. Finally, after marking the last paper, he made his call to Antonio to come pick him up to go to the mall. Antonio arrived a short while later, and once in the car, Daunte popped open two bottles of Moet he had grabbed from the cooler at home. The two men drank quickly as they headed to the freeway.

"It's time for some new hoes," Antonio said, sounding bored.

"I feel that. I'm about to get rid of all my old bitches and start new," Daunte replied as he downed the rest of his bottle.

They arrived at Somerset Mall and shopped for about two hours before they made their way to North Park Mall. North Park Mall was a small, ghetto mall on the outskirts of the city.

The mall police sometimes drove through the parking lots and picked out random cars to make sure their plates matched. They also checked to see if the owner owed the city for tickets. The only reason Daunte and Tony came to this mall was because of the fine women who shopped and worked there. They dreaded going to the other mall in Dearborn. The rent-a-cops there constantly followed and harassed you if you were young and black. A couple of years back, a black man was murdered in front of his family by a group of relentless mall security cowards who accused the man's daughter of stealing, when she did not.

After they parked, Daunte, still buzzed, was on every girl that walked past him in the shopping mall parking lot. By the time they were ready to leave, Daunte had pocketed a good twenty numbers. He also ran into one of his old girlfriends, who lured him into the men's shoe and clothing store, City Ballers, and bought the player a pair of midnight blue gators and a pair of cream gator tennis shoes. That would complete his collection of exotic gators until the new ones came out in the spring. Daunte promised he would have dinner with her after she had taken him shopping, but that promise would never be kept. Daunte was on top of his game, while Antonio followed slightly behind. Antonio was seven of ten while Daunte was around twenty something and zero.

They headed toward the car when Daunte spotted what he anticipated would be his last quest at the mall. To him, this girl was definitely baby mama material. She was light-skinned with long, curly hair and a Coke bottle shape. She was thick as hell like a video model. She wore a tight-fitting Rocawear cropped sweater top, accentuating her large, rounded, perky breasts. She must not have been wearing a bra because her sweater exposed her hardened nipples. Her body was too sexy, and from a distance her jeans looked painted on. Antonio was also impressed by the woman's splendor. She became an object of desire to him as well. He believed Daunte had stepped on his toes too many times today. Daunte would grab a girl and get her number before Antonio had a chance to decide if he wanted to talk to her or not. So now was his turn. This shorty was too fine to pass up.

As Daunte made it closer to the cover girl, she was even more beautiful up close. She had impeccable Indian-yellow skin with big chestnut brown eyes that seemed to be fixed on Antonio as Daunte approached. Both men noticed her admiration, causing Daunte's speed to slow down while Antonio's accelerated. Her expression of interest in Antonio was obvious.

"My name is Pretty Tony. How are you doing?" Antonio asked the curly haired bombshell.

"I'm fine. You look so familiar to me. I think I've seen you a couple times at Club Downtown. Oh, my name is Faith. I'm sorry for being rude," she said as she shifted her shopping bags to her left hand and reached out with the right one to shake his hand.

Daunte stood off to the side to allow Speedy Gonzalez to wrap up the bullshit.

"What's up playaaas?" a deep voice yelled from somewhere behind them.

Tony and Daunte's heads snapped in unison only to be greeted by Burnt Out Pete. They could tell he'd been drinking, and his swagger was a bit off as he stumbled toward the threesome.

"Burnt—I mean—Pete, what's crackin', man?" Tony turned to Daunte and rolled his eyes.

"Looks like y'all ma'fuckas got you a new juicy piece," Pete looked at Faith as he grabbed his crotch.

"Pete, man, this is Faith. We just met her and it's not going down like that," Daunte assured him.

Faith jumped in, playing it like she was a lesbian. "Yeah, I was just telling these two gentlemen how me and my girlfriend were out shopping for some new kitchen supplies."

Pete scratched his head with a dumfounded look on his face. Then it seemed like he snapped. "What the fuck eva. Y'all know you just leaving a ma'fucka out again. Shit, if she's a lesbo, I wanna watch."

Daunte knew he had to take care of business before things got ugly. "Pete, man, let me holla at you for a minute."

Daunte pulled Pete to the side to talk some sense into him while Antonio and Faith continued their conversation.

After much convincing, he finally got Pete to leave. He strolled back over to Faith and Antonio.

"Your hair is so pretty," Faith said to Antonio right before she reached out and touched it. "Wow, your hair is as long as mine," she continued. "You should let me braid it. You would look so sexy with braids."

That shit was about to make Daunte puke. He didn't want to stand there and hear that corny-ass shit, so he decided to ask Antonio for the keys so he could wait in the car.

"You're just going to leave your boy with a strange female? You don't know, I could be a rapist or something," Faith said playfully.

But Daunte didn't really believe in playful. To him, playful meant he was being flirted with, which made him conclude that it was over for the competition. In just a matter of seconds, Daunte knew Faith was the type of woman who liked niggas to remain a challenge, as he did with the women he met. Antonio was all in her personal space too soon. He was behaving how females often acted around men.

Antonio seemed to have forgotten the rule of *Time Out* that he and Daunte frequently passed out to women like candy. A *Time Out* was a temporary or permanent hold on communications with a person. The deception of it was to appear still interested as one slowly cut off communication. Whether it was cutting down the amount of time on the phone with that person, the number of e-mails exchanged, or how much time was spent together, the *Time Out* could come in many forms. Then hopefully, if the muthafucka ain't crazy, he would leave you alone...until when, and if, you were ready to ever give him another chance. Antonio was unaware that Faith had just flicked him a *Time Out*.

"My nigga ain't worried about you being a rapist! You seem too much like a retard to do something that serious," Daunte said while laughing.

"What you mean? I seem slow? You better watch it, because I bet that I can beat ya' ass!" Faith replied, laughing back with Daunte.

"Take your cap and that silly ass doo-rag off so I can see how you look," Faith demanded.

"I'm straight. I'm not black and Puerto Rican so I don't have all that good hair like you have to show off, Ms. Lopez."

"Oh! I see you got jokes. How did you know what I was mixed with? Everyone else always assumes that I'm just Hispanic." Faith seemed impressed.

"I got my secrets," Daunte replied.

"If you don't tell me now, then you have to tell me tonight, over dinner," Faith demanded.

To Antonio's ego, her statement was like the blow that knocked Joe Frazier out.

"If I'm free tonight, we can do dinner," Daunte said, smiling as they exchanged numbers and said their goodbyes.

Antonio was heated. Daunte did the same shit again—stepping on his muthafuckin' toes. He wanted to bust him in his muthafuckin' face so bad, but that would be sacrilegious to the code of being a player. Antonio didn't speak a word the whole ride to Daunte's house. Daunte didn't care. He wasn't about to baby Antonio's grown ass. There were plenty of nights when he got dissed and Antonio got lucky. Antonio pulled up to Daunte's house and made no attempt to speak or look at him.

"Nigga, what the fuck is wrong with you?" Daunte asked angrily.

"*You*, muthafucka, is the fuckin' problem! You're the worse muthafuckin' cock-blockin'-ass nigga that I've ever met in my life," Antonio retorted.

The two men bickered for several minutes before Daunte heard enough and exited the vehicle. Antonio burned rubber and then sped out of the subdivision like a madman.

***

Pete lingered in the mall parking lot for a while, watching Antonio and Daunte get their mack on with the so-called lesbian. After witnessing the exchange between Faith and the two men, Pete's face scrunched up like a madman.

"Those niggas don't know who they fuckin' with."

CHAPTER EIGHT

Daunte sat in the master bedroom of his two-thousand square foot house, wondering why his dawg was acting like a bitch. He noticed Antonio had changed ever since Daunte's Aunt Mattie had passed away and left him as the sole beneficiary of her $800,000 life insurance policy and the deed to her house. Daunte didn't grow up having a lot of money like Antonio. Daunte was pretty much brought up by his mom. His father left the scene when he was three-years-old. His mother, Leola, worked on the assembly line at a local plant and made all right money for a family of three, but there were seven of them. Along with Daunte and his mother, there was Yolanda, the oldest, and then there was Kirby, Kenny, Laurie, and his little brother, Angelo.

Growing up, Daunte and Antonio had their share of women. Antonio got the girls who liked the light-skinned boys with "good" hair. Daunte attracted the girls who liked boys of color with a little bit of street substance. They combined their efforts and learned how to conquer just about any woman.

In the neighborhood, Antonio was known by the girls as the cute and well-dressed one. His family had money. They would buy him the most expensive clothes. Now, as adults,

Daunte could afford to shop and buy the things that he wanted. At first his wardrobe wasn't a match for Antonio's, but he wasn't competing anyway. He just liked to dress. He was from Detroit, so style was embedded in him at a very young age. Antonio always liked to brag to Daunte about how much money he had until Aunt Mattie died and left Daunte her entire estate. Now Daunte had more clothes, a better house, a driveway full of expensive cars, and more investments than his dawg. Daunte owned a car wash, had a college degree, and claimed ownership in a Starbucks franchise that was being built in Flint, not to mention his substitute teaching gig. But Daunte never flaunted his new wealth or even talked about it.

Daunte used to pimp females for their money, but he had slowed down since he received his inheritance. He didn't send women to the street corners or hotels anymore to sleep with niggas. He made sure they had good jobs and went to work on time. So when it was payday he collected at least 80 percent of their checks. People couldn't understand how females could be so stupid. To him, they weren't stupid—they were just in love. He was a motivator, a coach, a teacher, and a friend. He played whatever role needed to manipulate them.

Antonio, on other hand, always had cash, so he never learned how to mack women for money. He wanted to know how, because that would make him look like a bigger playa. He hated the fact that he had the talent to gab, but unlike Daunte, he didn't have the gift to pimp. The ringing of Daunte's cell phone startled him. He had fallen asleep watching *The Usual Suspects*.

"Hello?"

"Hey, it's Faith. I met you and your boy, Pretty Tony, at the mall earlier."

Daunte, still half asleep, tried to recall who she was.

"Oh yeah, what's up, ma? How are you doing?"

"I'm fine. Were you sleeping? I can call you back some other time if you were."

"No, I'm cool. What's up for tonight?"

"Well, I'm kinda hungry and I was wondering if you would you like to go get something to eat?"

"That's cool, where do you want to go?"

"Right now I'm on campus in Ypsilanti, but tonight I'm spending the night at my parents' house in Farmington. So I thought that maybe we could go to Detroit and get some Pizza Papalis in Greektown," Faith suggested.

They both agreed Pizza Papalis would be cool and they would meet there at eleven.

Daunte showered and quickly got dressed. When he closed the door to his vehicle, his cell phone rang. It was Antonio, and he was sounding as if he still hadn't let the bullshit go.

"You still going to the club?" Antonio asked with no emotion or life in his voice. Daunte sat silently on the phone before replying.

"Naw, I'm on my way out."

"Word, where you headed?" Antonio asked with a little bit more emotion.

Daunte assumed Tony wanted to know if he was going out with Faith or not. He wasn't about to lie, so he told him.

"Aight, my nigga, just hit me up tomorrow. One," Antonio said with no visible feelings.

"One," Daunte replied and ended the call.

It was weird to be beefing with his best friend. During their eleven-year friendship, they had never argued this seriously over a female before. He wondered why Tony would start now, and why with her?

CHAPTER NINE

Faith Luciano was a few years younger than Daunte, but at the age of eighteen, she had already dated men twice his age. Being away at school had given her more freedom to do things she couldn't do at home. She was in was her freshman year at EMU, majoring in international business with a minor in American history. Faith was the oldest of three children. She had two younger sisters—Jessica, who was eleven, and Melissa, who was fourteen. Growing up, she had plenty of exposure to unhealthy relationships and the problems that came with them.

Faith's parents, Michael and Maria Luciano, were no match made in heaven. Mrs. Luciano would tell them that "Papa was a rolling stone" when they asked, "Where is daddy?" As a husband, Faith felt her father was terrible, but she believed that he was still a good dad. He was a strong provider and family man. He came to all of her dance recitals, he had never forgotten a birthday, and he had never missed any of her volleyball games. The only problem was that he would show up with women other than her mom. Faith was tired of hearing her mom crying over him in the middle of the night because he didn't come home or didn't even bother to call. Mr. Luciano often came home in the morning, telling his wife the same lame excuses like, "I was working late at the office," or "I fell asleep over the fellas' house after the game."

Faith wanted to tell her mother about her father's infidelities, but she didn't want to break her heart. Faith hated how her father was treating her mother, but she didn't want them to get a divorce. Even though her mama was a quiet Christian woman, there was still a strong possibility that she could wig out.

One Sunday morning, Mrs. Luciano decided that she and the kids would leave church early. Mr. Luciano was at home sick, and she couldn't help but to think about how pitiful he looked before they left. On their way back to the house, Mrs. Luciano stopped at the drug store and picked up a box of cold tabs, a bottle of orange juice, and a small jar of Vicks for her bed-stricken man. When they pulled up to the house, a purple Cadillac with plates that read MS2CUTE was parked in the driveway. Mrs. Luciano parked and exited her car as if she didn't even see the vehicle that was violating her parking space. She kept her composure, got out the car calmly, and opened the back door. She unbuckled Jessica, who was four at the time, from her car seat. She grabbed the bag of get-well goodies and proceeded to make her way up the steps of the porch. Faith and Melissa walked slowly behind their mother because they knew what waited behind those doors wasn't a surprise party from Daddy.

As Faith watched her mother unlock the front door, she wondered why her dad had chosen to be with other women besides her mom. Her mother still looked good. She was only in her late thirties and she didn't even look it. She was tall and light-skinned with long brown hair, blond highlights, and the prettiest puppy-dog eyes. She had a slender figure with a large chest and big butt to match. When Faith would go to the mall with her mom, a lot of young guys tried to hit on her, thinking that she was Faith's older sister, never imagining that she was actually her mother.

Before she married, Faith's mom was Maria Rodriguez, born in Puerto Rico. Her and her family moved to America when she was three-years-old. Her family relocated to Queens for ten years before moving to Florida. After high school, Maria went to a neighborhood community college and got her associate's degree in applied science. She wanted to go back to school for Fashion Management, but her interest in modeling had put that on the back burner.

To become a supermodel had been a dream of Maria's since she was a child, and who could better help her accomplish those dreams besides Michael Luciano, CEO and owner of Luciano Talent and Modeling Agency? Mr. Luciano had offices in Manhattan, Miami, L.A., Chicago, and Detroit. Michael played professional basketball for six years before he tore the ACL in his right knee during practice, which put his basketball career to an immediate end. Luciano invested in a couple of stocks that got lucky and he became a very rich man. That's how he was able to start his real estate and modeling agencies.

Michael loved Hispanic women, and they were the main reason he personally attended his talent searches in Florida and New York City. He was often mistaken as being Hispanic himself. People would walk up to him and just start speaking Spanish, but luckily he was fluent in Spanish and six other languages. When the six foot four, yella-skinned, medium built, goatee wearing, gigolo, with his hair pulled back into a ponytail, first met Maria, it was love at first sight. They courted for three months before they got married.

When Mrs. Luciano became pregnant with Faith, she put off her modeling career and became a full-time mom. When Jessica was born, Mr. Luciano's late nights at the office began. At first it started out as, "Baby I'm sorry. I just lost track of time," but it progressed to him coming home at three in the morning and sneaking in the bed, thinking Maria was still sleeping, but she wasn't. Eventually he started spending nights away from home, without even bothering to call.

On that Sunday, as Faith and her sisters looked on, Mrs. Luciano stood at her front door, thinking about about all the years of loyalty that she had given this man, and wondering how he had the nerve to bring one of his hoes to their house. Mrs. Luciano felt herself losing it as she opened the front door. She told the children to stay outside as she went in to investigate. Faith watched as her mom entered the house and a couple minutes later, she could hear things being broken as her mother cursed loudly in Spanish.

"¡La puta I sabe que usted no está durmiendo con mi marido!"

MS2CUTE ran out the house half-dressed as Mrs. Luciano gave chase. With one heel on and the other in her hand, the young home wrecker was able to outrun the twice her age attacker. Mrs. Luciano ran back in the house and raised hell with her husband until the devil was able to run loose. For weeks Maria didn't speak to Mr. Luciano. Mr. Luciano started coming home straight after work and was even cooking and doing some of the household chores. After a month had passed, she forgave him and allowed him back into the bedroom. As Faith expected, her dad went back to his old ways, and her mom once again went back to playing the fool.

Faith swore to herself that when she finally met that one guy who was special enough for her to give her all to, he would only have one time to fuck over her trust. Once that trust was broken, she would never again allow him another chance to break her heart.

CHAPTER TEN

Daunte arrived at the restaurant around quarter to eleven and was surprised to see Faith already seated. He spotted her sitting in the back booths by the bar. It seemed as though she had already attracted a few admirers. Some drunken dude staggered over from the bar to her table and before he could finish slurring his name, she stood up and gesticulated to Daunte.

"Hey, baby, I'm over here!"

The guy turned around, saw Daunte approaching, gave him a look of disgust, and mumbled something under his breath before he returned back to the bar where he planned to be all night. Faith smiled as Daunte made it to the table. She hugged him tightly, making sure all the other guys got the hint. They hugged in the middle of the aisle with what seemed like the whole restaurant watching. Daunte was tempted to grab her ass, but he didn't want to chance getting a negative reaction, so he gave up that thought. They sat down and began to converse.

"I like your braids. I figured you had them. You look very sexy with them," Faith said to Daunte, smiling from ear to ear.

She must think every cute guy that has braids is sexy, Daunte thought to himself.

"Sexy is not a good enough word to describe you," Daunte said while looking at her like she was the main course for the night.

"Hey, you're a lucky man. I could have been out clubbing with my girls tonight. So don't make me regret going out with you by doing something crazy. I carry Mace, and looking at your size, I think I could kick yo' ass," Faith said playfully.

"OK! Of course you can beat my ass. You're built like a man—you ole Xena the Warrior Princess lookin' muthafucka."

"Oh, that was kinda harsh, but you're just scared because you know that I can whip you," Faith added jokingly.

"Nigga, please. I would test you, but I don't want to mess up that pretty face."

"Please do not use that word around me. I hate it when my people call each other that word. I'm not trying to be fussy, but I'm not one, and would just prefer not to be called that," Faith advised.

"OK! OK! I will try to watch it around you," Daunte said sincerely, caught off guard by her changing mood.

They got into a debate on how ignorant it was for black folks to be calling each other "nigga."

"When we're at work, we don't go around the office using it to white people who probably don't want us working there in the first place, but we find it necessary to greet our friends and loved ones with it?" Faith said.

By the end of the debate, he decided that he was going to try to cut down his usage, but he told her it would be hard. Shit, he had been exposed to the word since he was a baby in the hospital, when his dad slapped his mom while she was recovering from labor, because Daunte was a different complexion than his father.

"That baby too light. That nigga ain't mine!" Smack!

But shit, he wasn't about to tell her that.

They realized after the debate was over that they hadn't ordered yet. The waitress came up and apologized for the long wait. She explained that since it was a Sunday night they hadn't expected it to be so busy. But the waitress's duties couldn't have been too demanding, because she had enough time to keep staring at Daunte.

"I think I already know what I want," Faith said, looking at Daunte as she put her hands on top of his.

The waitress took their orders and rolled her eyes at Faith as she walked off. After dinner, they stayed for a while, talking and having a couple of drinks. Faith insisted that she had to go home because she had a ten o'clock class in the morning. Like her, Daunte also had a way of convincing others to listen, so it didn't take long for her to give in to a trip to his yacht. She followed him for about five minutes, traveling south on E. Jefferson, then turning right on St. Auburn, leading to the Riverfront Yacht Club. She had told Daunte she could only stay for a minute, but that would be all he needed to convince her to stay until the morning.

You

Caught up like Anita Baker in your rapture
Your smile brings liberty like the statue
About your style and grace I can write
at least two chapters
For you, the London Bridge
I would conquer and capture
and name it after you
Comparing you to other women
is like comparing an atomic bomb to a firecracker
That's why your foes are afraid to attack you
Even the ones that are known for fronting
will back you
You are the first to my heart
like the first written gospel is to St. Matthew
What good is it for a man to have everything
but lack you?

CHAPTER ELEVEN

Daunte's yacht had 121 square feet of open cockpit space. The 4300 convertible incorporated design could be found on each Tiara yacht, and Daunte's had a super smooth, long-lasting, mirror-gloss finish with a no-skid surface. It also had a tilt-away helm with wide walkways and hand grabs. The living room was spacious and displayed a hand-stacked flagstone entertainment wall with leather chairs and textured fabrics that gave the room a warm, inviting feeling. The dining room was very detailed, with a lighted ceiling that highlighted the textured silk and lacquered chairs. The framed gigantic *Godfather* poster gave the room a dramatic dining experience.

Faith toured the boat as it set sail. She was so excited. She had only seen boats like this on TV. She hoped Daunte was not into anything illegal because she knew he couldn't afford things like this on a teacher's salary. Daunte dimmed the lights on the boat, undressed himself, and stepped into the Jacuzzi with a bottle of chardonnay.

"You can join me if you like. And don't worry, I have seen naked women before. There are some towels on the chair, and could you please grab two glasses from the bar?" Daunte asked as he soaked in the hot tub.

"Is there anything else you need, master, while I'm up? I thought you wanted me to get naked and join you? You can do that stuff yourself while I'm getting undressed," Faith replied as she began to slide her pants off.

Daunte didn't hesitate to get out and grab the glasses and towels. He felt her watching him as he walked to light some candles with his penis swinging freely. They both entered the Jacuzzi at the same time, staring at each other's goods as if they were in the fifth grade and this was their first time seeing the anatomy of the opposite sex.

"This is really romantic! I must admit, you're kind of debonair. I would hate it if you were involved in some type of illegal activity," she said jokingly, but at the same time letting him know if he was, she didn't want to have any part of it.

Before he would let her worries ruin the mood, Daunte reached over to kiss her. Her lips accepted and allowed his tongue to intertwine with hers. He kissed her passionately on her neck and then lifted her breasts out of the water and began to molest them with his tongue. He placed one supple breast in his mouth and began sucking it slowly while gently biting down on her nipple. That really turned her on.

Faith grabbed him by the head and began to carve her nails into his back as he got on top of her. She sucked his bottom lip as she grabbed his penis and tried to put it inside her. As bad as he wanted to be in her, feeling all her juices, he couldn't do it. He wouldn't do it. He moved her back and reached out of the Jacuzzi to grab the Magnum that he left in the pocket of his pants. She looked at him curiously to see why he had stopped. Daunte opened the condom and tossed the wrapper on the floor. After what looked like a quick masturbation session, the condom was on and he slid back into position.

Faith moved him off her and pushed him to the other side. Daunte sat with his back against the wall of the tub waiting for her next move. Faith wrapped her legs around him as her body floated. In a slow circular motion, he began to place himself inside her. She began moving and grinding, and Daunte reacted with a pounding after each one of her movements. He lifted her up by the waist and began to long dick her until her legs lost strength and just dangled from the air. He sat her down and positioned her so she could follow him. She gathered some energy as she followed him to the deck of the boat.

Luckily for Daunte, it was an Indian summer night, because otherwise she wouldn't have followed him outside. Daunte pushed her against the rail and poured champagne over her as he licked it from every inch of her body. He sucked it from her breasts, down to her navel, and ending at her inner thighs. He turned her around and began to enter her from the back. She felt him slide in slowly, with his strong hands gripping her hips as he rocked her back and forth. The pleasure was so intense that she could barely keep her eyes open as she tried to look out at the water to admire the view of the nightlife. The lights of the downtown office buildings and the "Welcome to Canada" sign brightened Lake Michigan. The night was quiet, and all that could be heard was the splashing of the waves against the boat and the clapping of their bodies as he moved in and out of her, followed by her screams of pleasure.

The sun was already beginning to rise when they finally collapsed from exhaustion. Only an hour had passed when Faith woke up, frantic. She had a ten a.m. class and didn't have any idea what time it was. She knew that she had to get Daunte up and have him return back to shore. She turned over in the bed to wake him, only to find that he wasn't there. He entered the bedroom carrying a breakfast tray with two plates of hotcakes and a pitcher of freshly squeezed orange juice.

"I have some clean clothes for you to put on once you're out of the shower. Don't worry. It's only eight a.m. and we'll be back at the boathouse in about twenty minutes," Daunte said as he handed her the food.

She ate hurriedly and showered. By the time she got dressed, they were already docked. She kissed him goodbye and promised that she would call him when she got a chance.

Faith was a remarkable woman. Daunte had never felt this way about anyone before and it was weird to him because it was their first date. Was this the woman he had been waiting for? She was perfect to him. She was beautiful, smart, witty, and ghetto. For the first time in his life, he believed that he could be faithful to a woman if he chose to. He hoped she wouldn't turn out to be a freak. She did try to have sex with him without a rubber, but maybe she just wasn't thinking at the time. Nevertheless, he was interested, and he would pursue her until fate determined otherwise.

She Is

She's a dime piece fo' sho'
Smile shines like soul glo
Looks so cold, to be around her
you have to dress like an Eskimo
Sent her mama a thank you letter,
because what she has created for the world
is exceptional
It would have been a compliment, except she knows
She has more style than an international fashion show
Body so hot, when she walks
her footsteps melt the snow
Her eyes are paralyzing, gaze too deep
they'll grab you and won't let you go
Her beauty strings beings and leave minds
like the vegetable
Black and Puerto Rican, damn she got the best of both
She's so fine, she turn gay niggas back to heterosexuals
Her lips is so sexy it makes every word she speaks
seem so sexual
Not only irresistible, she's Fine, Young, & Intellectual
Her presence alone is inspirational,
That's why when niggas is around her
like professional weed smokers at a Jamaican festival,
they hate to go
Her essence has turned my words
into a mellifluous flow
Detonated my lyrical thinking and left my mind
set to blow
She stayed picked out of the competition like a 70s 'fro
She's a 2005 BMW Z8 convertible on 22s
with a candy coat

That's why the competition hate on her without justice
like the State of Florida
during the last presidential election,
when black folks came out to vote.

CHAPTER TWELVE

Daunte decided to call Antonio to see what was up. He wasn't going to allow their friendship to be destroyed over a female.

"Hello," Antonio answered.

"Look, dawg, I want to squash this bullshit. My bad if you think I stepped on your toes, but I'm feeling this girl. I think she might be the one, my nigga. I mean, playa."

"What? Anyway, *nigga*, it's all good, but don't get too attached to her. Most females who are able to get playas to settle down are normally the ones who will eventually have them on their knees, begging like a lost puppy."

***

"Girl, I couldn't believe it," Faith said to Monica, her girlfriend, as they talked in class.

"Girl, that don't even sound like you, sleeping with a guy on the first night," Monica replied low enough for only Faith to hear.

They were early to class and there were only two other people in there, but they were busy in their own conversation.

"I hope he don't think I'm a ho or something," Faith said, looking for advice from her girl.

"Shit, that fool would have to be crazy to think something like that. Far as I heard this is the first time that you have ever slept with a guy on a first date and how long have I known you?" Monica asked as the women laughed. "Girl, don't get me started!"

"I know, girl, you're right," Faith agreed.

Professor Chaney came into class and began writing on the chalkboard which chapters they were going to cover for the week. The class filled up quickly, so the ladies had to put their discussion on hold until later.

***

Daunte pulled up to his cousin Dot's house. She wanted to use his camcorder to tape her son's birthday party. He came by to drop it off before heading up to EMU to see Faith. She had called him earlier and invited him over for dinner. Daunte rang the doorbell to his older cousin's townhouse. She was his favorite cousin. They would talk all the time about life, money, and relationships. She would tell him about the men problems that she frequently had and he would brag to her about how many women he had slept with that week.

His little cousin Jo Jo answered the door. Dot was back in the kitchen frying chicken for the kiddy disco. She had her Mary J. Bilge CD banging so loud that she couldn't hear the doorbell chimes over the beats of "Family Affair." Daunte caught Dot by surprise, trying to Harlem Shake, but it looked more like she was having a seizure.

"Hey, cuz!" Daunte said, laughing.

"Oh my goodness, boy, don't do that shit!" Dot yelled after being startled. "You almost got that pretty face of yours scorched!" Dot said while turning the chicken over as grease popped from the skillet.

Daunte told her about Faith and how he thought she was different from all the girls that he had been messing with. To Dot, it seemed like every time Daunte came over, there was always a new girl he liked. By his next visit, there would be somebody new because he got bored with the last one. So Daunte telling Dot about Faith just went in one in ear and out the other.

CHAPTER THIRTEEN

The door rattled and unlocked as the guy behind the desk buzzed Daunte in. There were young white kids all over the place, some checking their mailboxes while others sat in small study groups in the lobby. Daunte pulled out his sheet of paper with the directions Faith had given him. Her dorm room was on the second floor in room 2336C.

Go up to the second floor, make a left, and walk all the way down the hall until you see the fire sign exit. My room is two doors before that exit.

Daunte went up the stairs, passing the first floor and stepping over a kissing couple who blocked the stairwell. He made a left when he came to the second level. He was surprised to see the posters of Justin Timberlake and Britney Spears that were plastered all over the walls and doors. Daunte had gone to an HBCU, so he was only used to seeing Bob Marley and Tupac posters. He was accustomed to smelling incense and walking past open dorm rooms seeing somebody getting their hair braided while they studied.

Daunte walked further down the hall past the posters to what he assumed was the black section of the dormitory. You could hear a Dr. Dre beat banging in the hallway. Daunte didn't see any Bob Marley or Tupac posters, just clippings of expensive trucks. A few people had put up a picture of themselves on their door next to their message pads. As he made his way to his destination, he stopped to view a photo that some female had posted of herself on the door. His admiration quickly turned into embarrassment when Faith peeped her head out of her room, which was a couple of doors down.

"You lost, boo boo?" Faith asked, catching him by surprise.

Faith stepped out of her dorm room, showing off her blue jean miniskirt set. With each step she took it seemed as if her breasts were going to pop the single button on her top that held them in. She hugged him as if she hadn't seen him in years, but he had to quickly let her go because he felt himself getting too excited. Faith blushed as he followed her back into her room. She had been lucky enough to get a single, but she did have a suitemate to share the bathroom with. She had a gigantic poster of Morris Chestnut over her twin-sized bed, and on her dresser she had a framed picture that she had taken with Fat Joe at the Puerto Rican Day Parade earlier that year. Her room was decorated with unopened scented candles and a gallery of club pictures, and her bed was buried under stuffed Tweety birds and textbooks.

Faith made room for Daunte to sit down on the bed before she went down the hall to make his plate. She had used the dorm's kitchen to make spaghetti for him. Daunte loved it. It was a little watery, but it was still good. After dinner, they cuddled and watched a movie before Daunte made his way back home.

We

Your body is mad tight
Can't believe I didn't try to fuck
The sex was on fire but it's your mental
that got me stuck
Is this fate or pure luck?
About you I'm so excited
that I have to tell people from Europe
Love, I had placed on the bench, but now you're up
How do I go from a playa to being faithful
when I used to make women's eyes blur up?
Your presence causes my poetic thinking to stir up
We belong together
like high top fades and the 80s phrase
"Word Up!"

CHAPTER FOURTEEN

Two Years Later

Faith had moved off campus and now lived with Daunte. In the beginning they were inseparable. They did everything together—Cedar Point, comedy jams, grocery shopping. You name it and they were together, doing it. There was a remarkable confluence in their thinking. They thought the same way about everything. Antonio hated the fact that Faith was taking all of Daunte's time away from him.

Recently Faith had suggested to Daunte that they should move to New York. She was graduating early because she had attended summer classes and was thinking about going to law school there. Antonio became furious when Daunte told him that he had been applying for a teaching position in Manhattan, especially now that Faith was treating his nigga like a sucker. She would hang out all night, and then bitch at Daunte if he wanted to go out with Antonio and the fellas. Antonio could see a change for the worse in his best friend since he had started dating Faith. His confidence level was at an all time low. She castigated him for trying to be a teacher. She often told him that he should leave his vernacular for the streets and use proper English in the classroom.

"We don't want our future generation to grow up sounding like you, do we?"

Teaching was in Daunte's heart. It obviously wasn't for the money. It was a passion that he felt. Antonio was also upset because Faith wasn't complaining about what Daunte did for a living when she needed money to go shopping. Daunte had never bought a female shit, but now he was spending his money on this overpriced ho. Besides all of that, Daunte was making Antonio look bad, because word got back that Daunte was pussy whipped and was getting suckered by some Spanish chick for all his loot. So Antonio decided he would save their reputation himself, at whatever cost.

***

On this day, Antonio came by to pick up Daunte. He wanted him to ride with him over to some chick's crib before they went to work out. They pulled up to a shabby looking apartment building on the northwest side of Detroit. There were schoolgirls in front of the building, playing hopscotch and jumping rope. It was getting dark so you could hear their parents yelling for them to come inside from the windows of the 2005 *Good Times* looking projects. At least three crack heads had approached and asked for change before Antonio and Daunte could walk into the building.

The front door remained unlocked because someone had jammed it with paper, so people entered as they pleased. The lobby was filled with drug addicts and sleeping winos. Antonio knocked on apartment E12 and a young brown-skinned female who looked no older than nineteen opened the door. She wore a Playboy bunny tube top with some daisy duke shorts that went up her ass. She let them in, and surprisingly her apartment was decently clean. It seemed as if they had just entered a totally different apartment complex. Antonio said that he had met her while she stood waiting for the bus to go to her classes at college. What Antonio had failed to mention was that she was also a stripper at Detroit Hot Girls.

No sooner than Daunte had taken a seat, she turned on the booty shaking music and began wiggling just about every inch of her body in his face, wearing nothing but a g-string. She turned with her ass cheeks bouncing in his face before giving him a lap dance. Daunte could feel temptations starting to rise.

Daunte and Faith hadn't had sex in two weeks because he still wanted to use a condom. Faith thought that he must be fucking around since he was so scared to have sex with her without protection. He told her if they both went and got tested, they could ditch the rubber. She received her negative results a month ago and Daunte hadn't attempted to see a doctor yet, so now she was holding back completely until he stopped procrastinating.

"Damn, bitch, get off of me!" Daunte said, pushing the stripper off him and onto the floor. "Dawg, I can't believe you brought me over here for this bullshit. Man, what the fuck is wrong wit' you? I love Faith. I told you that I'm not into this type of shit anymore. This is the third time you tried some shit like this!"

"Melanie, go into the bedroom. I'll be there in a minute," Antonio told the teenager.

"Look, I just wanted you to have a little fun, but I see you acting like a lil bitch right now. So I'll be back, *playa*. I'm about to get me some pussy—something you haven't had, my nigga, in a couple of weeks," Antonio said as he headed to the bedroom.

After a couple hard thumps against the wall, followed by the young girl's vociferous screams, Antonio reappeared, smiling and fastening his belt.

"Ain't nothing like a quickie before a good workout," Antonio said, laughing.

They were in the car when Daunte asked Antonio to come with him to get tested.

"Tested for what?"

"For AIDS, muthafucka. We can go to my doctor. I know he's there until seven p.m. It will only take about thirty minutes, then we can go work out. The results will come by mail in a couple of days."

"Aight, nigga, but the only reason you doing this shit is so you can finally get some pussy," Antonio said after he agreed.

"And you know this, man!" Daunte played along, but he really was getting tested because he was tired of not knowing what the results might be. Seeing Antonio still having careless sex had reminded him of what he needed to do.

CHAPTER FIFTEEN

After they left Dr. Johnson's office, Antonio dropped Daunte off. They would have to put their workout on hold until tomorrow because Antonio had received another booty call from a sister on the eastside. Daunte entered the house and found Faith asleep on the couch. He sat next to her and began stroking her hair. Faith awakened, looking upset.

"Where have you been?"

"Me and Antonio went to Dr. Johnson's so we could get tested like I told you."

Faith twisted her lips, then closed her eyes and returned back to sleep.

"What the hell? Aw naw, get yo ass up," Daunte said as he tried to put his hand up her shirt to unfasten her bra.

She grabbed his hand with a Jackie Chan karate move and they began to wrestle, with Daunte allowing himself to lose.

"You got some weed?" Faith asked.

"Yeah. I only got enough for one blunt. Why, you wanna' smoke?"

"Yeah, man, I've been feeling stressed all day," Faith replied.

Daunte rolled the last of the weed he had left in the red sandwich bag that he had bought from Pete last week.

"I'm going to page Burnt Out Pete to bring me an ounce this time so I don't have to keep paging his ass all the time," Daunte said as he picked up the phone.

"Why do you guys always call him Burnt Out Pete?" Faith asked.

"Everybody do. It's just a nickname that the 'hood gave him back in the day."

"Oh," Faith said as Daunte passed her the blunt.

Faith had a low tolerance for weed. She rarely smoked, so she must have been really stressed to do it on a school night.

"Hey, what's up with a freestyle battle?" Faith asked out of nowhere.

"What's up wit it, but I'm tellin' you, don't get mad if I embarrass you."

Faith waited until the blunt was the size of a cigarette butt before she decided she couldn't hit it anymore. Daunte took one last puff and then extinguished the flame. Faith got up and put on an instrumental and then proceeded to flow:

Um....check...1...2, are you ready?
Me and my man, smoking and chillin'
You to me baby, is so appealin'
With you is all that I'm dealin' Mr. Man of Steelin' Shit... hey I
can be for real...
you know baby I got that whip appeal
It can give you chills and show you thrills
Hey...um...I don't know what else to say...
I'm just rappin' anyway...um... hey...
Why don't you take the mic and show me
what you gotta say

Faith laughed as she passed the remote control that she was using as a mic to her male counterpart. Daunte stood up, towering over her with the remote palmed in his right hand as if he was about to perform in a live concert. With his other hand, he grabbed and held her hand like she was an offstage fan as he began his cadence flow.

When it comes to this rap shit,
Baby girl I should be crowned the master
While you should be crowned queen, because your face is so beautiful it should be the relief of our nation's unnatural and natural disasters
I'm goin' to put it like this, baby you're too hot
You got me juiced like to Tupac
By other niggas, you used to be handcuffed
but like Rerun I pop locks
Me and you are a deadly mix to swallow
like Pepsi and Pop Rocks
Your body so pulverizing, it can dismantle the block
You are wanted more by niggas, than a fugitive
by the police, who shot cops
Your love is so fertile
it can cause my lyrical mind to grow crops
Everywhere you go, you show stop
You got more flavor than a rainbow of Blow Pops Beauty so pure it could end the holy war
out of the pimp game, you got me sold out
like concert tickets when Prince is on tour

"Damn! You was goin' on for a minute! What you say, I got more flavor than a rainbow of Blow Pops? That shit was tight!" Faith said, hugging on Daunte, laughing and smiling.

Out of nowhere the telephone rang and startled the amorous couple.

"Let me get that. It might be Pete," Daunte said, reaching for the cordless.

"I'm already high. I don't need any more tonight. Just let the answering machine get it," Faith pleaded. She wrapped her arms back around him as the answering machine picked up.

"Sorry we're not able to take your call right now. Please leave a message after the tone and we'll get back to you shortly."

Beep. Beep. Be---ep.

"Hey Daunte, this is Crystal. I was just thinking about you. I haven't heard from you in a while. This girl in my class named Melanie called me today and asked me if I had the notes for Business Law. Somehow we got into this conversation about how many fine niggas there are in Detroit, and she mentioned to me that this guy named Pretty Tony had come by with his boy, Daunte, today. I was like, girl, I know them. She said that she tried to give you a lap dance, but you pushed her off of you and made her hurt her knee. I thought that shit was so funny! That's good that you did that, cause she ain't nothin' but a ho anyway. Hey, give me a call at 313-555-7472 when you get this. Maybe we could hook up like old times. Talk to you soon, sexy."

Click.

It was like an atomic bomb had just launched as they sat and listened in disbelief. When it finally landed, Faith exploded in fury.

"I can't believe it, you lying muthafucka. How could you do this to me?" Faith cried with tears shattering down her face like glass dropping and breaking into a thousand pieces.

Daunte tried to explain, but she didn't want to hear his rebuttal. Faith ran up the stairs and started packing her things. Daunte went upstairs after her, trying to console her, but was greeted with an open-handed smack. His temper flared as this time her right hand came around and struck him again. He quickly shook off his anger and tried reasoning with her.

"Please, just listen!" Daunte begged of her.

"Leave me alone. Somebody help!" Faith yelled as she became vehement in her screaming.

Daunte finally convinced her to stay by telling her that he would leave the house long enough for her to calm down.

"Go then. Get the fuck out!" Faith screamed to him while ballin' on the ground like a hurt child.

Daunte grabbed his car keys and left. He didn't understand why the fuck Crystal had called him after all that time, or why he was leaving his own house for Faith's high ass to calm down. It was bad enough that they were already going through problems. Daunte believed this situation was going to permanently damage their relationship, if not become the death of it.

Changed

How do I look fuckin' wit someone else, I'm hooked
The flight is booked, my attention span is took
Your class knocks niggas' off their feet
like the ground just shook
Don't get upset about that groupie
I already gave her the boot,
now I see...I should have left the foot
You are all that I need and all that I dream
Other women are mere peasants,
who can't intervene
and come between a King and his Queen
By that chickenhead, I know you can't be fazed
You're the only one that got me amazed
So heavy that it can't be weighed
After spending time with you, for days I daze
I know at times I kept you at bay
but I still want you to stay
I'm tired of niggas asking me where the hoes at
I'm a faithful man now, shorty,
and you've helped me expose that
Like a Kodak picture, my word, you can hold that
Your heart has retired my jersey
and it I would never throw back
While your trust is like an asthmatic fat kid,
six feet away from his birthday candles
it's impossible for me to blow that
Me cheating on you now would never happen
like 360 waves on Kojak
My words are like Jeopardy trivia
I'm giving you the answers before the questions
because my true thoughts of you,

I wanted you to know that
Let's sit on the balcony
overlooking the city's nightlights
As I rap to you in a slow flow format
I never had a girl that I could kiss, adore, and dap
Freaks and hood rats don't miss no more of that
I would hate to lose a silver dollar over a few pennies
Even if I had Bill Gates's money,
I couldn't afford that.

CHAPTER SIXTEEN

Daunte came home around five in the morning. He had gone by Dot's place and fallen asleep on the couch. He woke up from a bad dream and realized it was almost daybreak. On his way to the house, he couldn't understand why this was happening. He hadn't cheated on Faith during their whole two-year relationship. Yeah, he may have gotten a couple of phone numbers, but he really wasn't going to call them.

It wasn't like she was free from sin. She became inflexible when he wanted to go out with his boys. She would throw fits and act like he was committing a crime. When she went out with her girls, she didn't ask him for permission—she just left. But when he just left, she acted like he was abandoning her. She thrived on attention and needed somebody to baby her constantly. So when she couldn't get that from Daunte, she called her ex, who was so obsequious that he would do and say anything that she wanted to try to get her back. She swore that she didn't talk to him anymore.

One day Daunte got the phone bill with the nigga's number on there. It showed the dates she had called, and how long the calls lasted. One time she talked to that nigga for three hours. Daunte was pissed off. She was in his house and on his phone, making long distance calls to a nigga she used to fuck. Daunte started to kick her ass out then, but like Dot said, it could have just been harmless conversation. Besides, Faith had found six numbers in his pocket that same day. Even though he wanted to curse her out, he knew he really couldn't say shit.

Daunte walked upstairs to see if Faith was still home. He tried to open the bedroom door, but it was locked. Daunte went back downstairs, frustrated, but relieved at the sight of the red baggie with weed in it. He split open a green leaf and there was just enough weed left in the Ziploc for him to roll a decent blunt. He went into the guest bedroom, blazed, and watched cable until he fell asleep.

***

Daunte awakened to find that Faith had already left. He tried calling her cell phone, but after several failed attempts, he finally gave it a rest. He showered and then dressed before he tried again. This time she answered.

"Hello?"

Daunte was relieved to hear her voice instead of her voicemail this time.

"Baby, I just..."

Faith sharply cut him off before he could finish, destroying all hopes that he had held about them being able to finally communicate.

"Daunte, I'm tired of your bullshit. This is the last straw. I think maybe I need to test the waters and see what else is out there for me. I just need a break."

This was something Daunte recalled women having told their boyfriends when they would sneak out to be with him.

Daunte felt his situation was different because he wasn't cheating on Faith. What happened to those niggas didn't pertain to him.

"We don't need to take a break. We're just going through a rough spot right now."

"Daunte, I don't feel the same about you anymore. I love you, but I'm not in love with you," Faith said softly, but fiercely enough to get her point across.

Daunte's heart dropped. He tried to explain that everything would be how it was before. He had another flashback of how females sounded when they pleaded for him to stay, but quickly shook it off and continued what he would have considered begging.

"Please, baby, don't do this."

"Fine, you want me to stay, I'll stay. I just won't tell you when I'm fuckin' someone else, since you whinin' and shit," Faith said as a ton of bricks fell on Daunte's ego.

Daunte sat on the phone in silence.

"So we're over, right?" Faith asked disdainfully.

Daunte, heartbroken, answered with a simple yes.

"Good, I'll be moving out in about a week or two, but for the next couple of days, I'll be at my parents."

The phone clicked and died in Daunte's ear. A female acquaintance of Daunte's once told him that one day he was going to meet a female who would bring him as much heartache as he had brought to so many others. And now Faith was that female.

Insanity

In your eyes, how do you see me?
Why do you stay and judge me?
Why can't you just leave me?
I'm sick of the pain that I can't seem to escape
and I'm sick of the rain, so just bring me my fate
Lord, give me the strength, so I can break free
How do I get away, when it's myself
who keeps me?
I'm sick of hearing her voice
because her words hinder my spirit
She knows how it feels to be out of love,
while I pray for the day that I can feel it
She no longer listens;
she says I'm just repeating myself
I swear this will be the last try, but every time
I just end up, mentally defeating myself
If you ever loved me, why would you let me go on
In believing you still love me?
you must want to destroy me
You must want to see
my sanity gone.

CHAPTER SEVENTEEN

The cab blew its horn impatiently as Daunte finally located his keys. He grabbed his luggage and the stack of mail that was piled in his mailbox. He had totally neglected to check it the last couple of days due to the bullshit that had been going on. One of the schools in New York that he had applied to for a teaching position had responded back. They offered to fly him to Manhattan for the weekend for an interview. His enthusiasm to move to New York had left since he and Faith had split up. Daunte decided that he was still going to make the trip, and he was on his way there now. He wanted to see what they were offering before he shut them out.

Before he met Faith, Daunte used to go visit his Uncle Mike in Brooklyn every other year. He also had cousins in Queens and a couple of Rican mamis in Spanish Harlem. The impetuous taxi driver pounded the horn once more as Daunte locked his front door.

"Damn, chill the fuck out, you ole Osama Bin Laden lookin' muthafucka!" Daunte exhorted as he rolled his Gucci suitcase to the yellow cab.

"Sorry, my friend. I wasn't sure if you heard me." The driver apologized once more as he put Daunte's things in the trunk.

Daunte didn't respond as he took his seat in the cab and examined the Middle Eastern man's identification that seemed to be absorbed in the bulletproof glass that it was attached to. On the way to the city airport Daunte began to go through his mail. It was pretty much the same junk mail—pre-approved credit applications, sales papers, and a stack of "miracle letters" from local evangelists.

Daunte opened one of the sales papers and a white envelope fell onto his lap. It was a letter from Dr. Johnson's office. Daunte's hands trembled in fear as he reached to pick it up. He had totally forgotten that he and Antonio had gotten tested. He wondered if Antonio had received his letter yet. If he had, he hadn't mentioned it when Daunte called and told him that he would be in New York for an interview over the weekend. Daunte thought back to all of the freaky-ass females he had slept with in his life. He thought about all the one-night stands that he had as well. He almost changed his mind about opening the letter.

Daunte had always told Antonio that he believed that they were cursed. Almost every female that they went out with would allow them to fuck the same day. Sometimes when Daunte was drunk, he would chance it without a condom if the girl said that she didn't have anything. Each time afterward, he knew that he could have just stuck his foot in the grave. Then he would pray to God and try to negotiate. If the Lord would keep him free of disease, he would "never" have unprotected sex again. So he knew that this letter could mean catch-up time for all the broken promises he had made and forgotten about.

Daunte's eyes became glossy as he began to read the letter of his uncertain fate. His heart pounded rapidly as the tears finally escaped from his lids that held them captive. The taxicab driver eyeballed him through the rearview mirror but didn't speak a word. Daunte wasn't afraid of death, but he was terrified of dying from AIDS. He unfolded the paper as his eyes scanned for a miracle. *Negative* in bold letters jumped from the correspondence as he skipped from the opening remarks to the results. Daunte was ecstatic. He began to wipe the tears from his eyes as he laughed like a madman.

"We have arrived!" the driver happily advised.

Daunte over-tipped the cabby and ran off to catch his plane to New York City. On the flight, all Daunte could think about were the results. He made a promise to God and himself that from that moment forward he was going to make a change for the better and give his life to Christ.

I Repent

Baby, I can't stop the fights
You were the torch of my life
that could light up the darkest night
Now you complain as much
as a group of weed heads
when the blunt ain't sparking right
and our arguments no longer barks, it bites
We used to always be together
like Mike and Ikes and swoosh and Nikes
But now you have no use to me like an NBA player
with no game or height
It just ain't making no sense to keep the pretense
We no longer have a dream house
just a burnt down picket fence
This bullshit you're running me is *played* out
like the musical *Rent*
If it is a sin to waste so much time,
then Lord, I repent.

CHAPTER EIGHTEEN

Faith listened to the message Daunte had left on her voicemail. He told her that he was going to be in New York for an interview until Sunday. She decided to go to the house and get some studying done since he wouldn't be there to bother her. Faith sat on the couch, talking to one of her classmates on the phone when the doorbell rang. She got up to answer the door with the phone still glued to her ear.

"Who is it?" Faith asked before looking out the peephole to see Antonio smiling outside the door like a snake.

"I'm going to call you back," Faith told the female who held on the line.

She clicked off the phone as Antonio rung the doorbell again.

"I heard you the first time," Faith said as she flung open the door, allowing Antonio to enter. He walked right past her and causally danced himself into the living room.

"How can I help you, Antonio?" Faith asked, trying to get on his nerves by addressing him by his real name.

"Where my nigga at?" Antonio inquired as he walked around the domain, making sure that they were alone.

"He's in New York," she responded sharply, knowing that he already knew that.

"For real? That nigga ain't tell me he was going to New York!"

"Look, I told you before about using that word around me. Please do not use it again in my house."

"Yeah...OK, you got it," Antonio replied, thinking to himself that this bitch had a lot of balls claiming that this was her house.

Faith had taken her seat back on the couch and began going over her notes from class.

"Hey, is it cool for me to chill here for a minute? I'm waiting for this shorty to call me back," Antonio explained, concealing his ruthless machinations.

Faith agreed to let him wait. Antonio walked over to the bar and made himself a drink. He poured himself a glass of cognac mixed with pop, and made her some vodka with a tap of Red Bull. Antonio had the heads up on what she drank because Daunte never stopped running his mouth about her.

"Have a drink with me?" Antonio asked her as he handed her the glass.

She looked at him suspiciously before she accepted the offering. After she took a couple sips, Antonio asked Faith if she could put some music on. She sighed for a brief moment before replying that she would put on a movie. She got up and put her notes on the coffee table. As she made her way to the television, Antonio gave a short whistle.

"OK, playboy, you better chill out. I think you must have made your drink a little too strong," Faith said while bending down and going through the box of DVDs.

As she searched, the black jogging pants that she wore slid down further, exposing her red thong.

"Are you finished staring at the crack of my ass?" Faith asked without turning around to catch him.

"Ain't nobody paying yo ass no attention."

Faith found the movie that she wanted to watch and loaded it in the DVD player. She returned back to her seat, smiling from ear to ear as *The Best Man* came on. When Faith first met Antonio, she thought he was very attractive, but she just wasn't feeling him. As time went by, the more she saw him, the more she found herself intrigued. She just recently began to wonder why she had chosen Daunte over him. She had always loved pretty boys. Daunte was sexy, but he was too ghetto for her. Faith almost felt weird being attracted to Antonio because he kind of reminded her of her father. Tonight, Faith felt like she had the opportunity to do what she had lately been fantasizing about.

Daunte tried to portray himself as if he wasn't a player anymore, but she found that hard to believe, even though she had never seen him do anything with her own eyes. The phone numbers that she kept finding were the only reason she decided that he was still a ho. Antonio, on the other hand, was Antonio. He didn't put up a front, and that's what she liked about him.

Faith turned and faced Antonio. She put her arms over his shoulders and placed her lips on his. He tried to kiss her, but her mouth didn't allow it. She just wanted to feel how his lips would feel on hers, which she now believed was a mistake because that made her want to take this sensation to the next level.

Faith clicked off the lights with the remote control and hit a couple of other buttons, making the TV turn off and the stereo system come on. The soulful music of Maxwell surrounded them as she closed her eyes and felt Antonio's tongue enter her mouth. She felt almost dizzy from the excitement of doing something so forbidden. Antonio undressed her quickly and within seconds he had slid himself inside her. Faith's faint voice asked him to put on a condom, but her request was denied, and in minutes, to her surprise, their sexual indulgence was over as quickly as it started.

"What the fuck was that?" Faith asked as she pushed him off her and stared at him in disgust. Antonio sat up and reached for his drink.

"Oh hell no, you better start eating my pussy or something," Faith demanded.

"Bitch, you must be crazy!" Antonio replied as he got up and started putting on his clothes.

Faith began yelling at Antonio as he walked toward the door, laughing out loud.

"You want to know what's funny? I actually thought that maybe you would be able to work that little muthafucka when you pulled it out. I should have told you no when I felt your little-ass dick, but I gave you the benefit of the doubt. What's the matter, Mr. Two-Minute Man? This pussy too wet for you? Now you know how I got your punk-ass boy whipped," Faith screamed. She quickly slammed the door shut when she saw that her comments had angered Antonio enough to turn back and head toward her on the porch.

After the door closed, he stood for a brief second on the steps, then turned around and headed for his vehicle as she watched from the blinds.

CHAPTER NINETEEN

The cab pulled out of the driveway as Daunte unlocked the front door to his house. It was Sunday and he was back from his trip to New York. He didn't get the teacher's position that he interviewed for because he was unable pass the surprise urine test. It was embarrassing for him when they told him that he didn't pass the drug examination. It was especially humiliating that he failed, being a black man applying for a teacher's position in a predominately white school district. He knew that one day, weed was going to hold him back from goals he wanted to accomplish.

After the rejection from the school, he decided it was time to give up smoking. To do so meant he would have to concentrate on all the negatives that weed brought him. Daunte got in touch with his peoples from uptown and was able to attend church with them before his six o'clock flight back to Detroit. Pastor Davis preached a very spiritual sermon that Sunday morning. Daunte sometimes hated going to his church back home because people were always gossiping, running around the aisles like track stars, and screaming at the top of their lungs as if their house had just caught fire. But something convinced him to go to church this day, and he was grateful that he had.

The pastor talked about how people were always grabbing books off the shelf and reading them for inspiration, instead of picking up the most inspirational book of all—the Bible.

"How can you save someone who is doing wrong when you haven't crucified your own flesh? Can somebody help me? I'm tired of always hearing people crying and whining. 'Why don't God give me a new job like Jane?' 'Why don't God give me nice clothes like Jimmy?' 'Why don't God give me a NEW BIG CADILIAC like YOU, PASTOR DAVIS!!' Does somebody hear me in here this morning? You must ask God to give you what you desire. He says to ask and you shall receive. You can't just hope things will get better. You have to get down on your knees and pray. Do you think you're too good for God? Are you too cool to kneel down on your eighty-dollar pair of designer jeans and ask his forgiveness? Or ask him for what you feel you deserve? Can I get a witness in here? I said, can I get a witness in here?

"Y'all ain't 'sleep this morning, is ya? Don't be afraid to ask your Savior for anything! Don't you know all things can be done through Christ? If you don't know the Lord, or you just want to rededicate yourself to Christ, then today is the day. Ask him for forgiveness and he will cleanse you. Please repeat this short prayer after me.

"If we confess our sins, he is faithful and righteous to forgive us our sins and to cleanse us from all unrighteousness.1 John 1:9

"O God, I need to feel that I have forgiveness from you. So often my good intentions do not become what I want them to be, and so often the good I want to do, I don't do. It is hard to face up to the wrong that is in my life. When I feel your forgiveness, I feel clean and good inside and so free to be what you want me to be. Help me feel this goodness and strengthen me to forgive those who have wronged me. I pray in the name of Christ who shows us the way to your forgiving presence. Amen."

The pastor's sermon brought an overwhelming joy to Daunte's heart. It had lifted his burdens and purified his soul. He confessed before the Lord and was born again.

When Daunte opened the front door to his home, he found that Faith was still not there. He checked the house for her things and sadness came upon him when he discovered that she had completely moved out. He knew it was probably for the best. The Lord had now given him the strength to move on, and he didn't need to contaminate his spirit or his house with all the fussing, cussing, and confusion anyway.

Daunte put his things down and noticed their photo album lying on the bed. He started laughing after he saw that she had cut her face out of all the pictures they had taken together.

Free At Last

As Mary Jane perishes in the arms of a parching Dutch
On paper, I try to analyze the question
"If the ones you love betray you,
then who can you trust?"
I didn't give this woman my heart,
I only allowed her to touch
Without warning she grabbed it and held it hostage
in her clutch
I thought it was love, but now that it is over
I realize we were just infatuated by lust
After you have sex with someone so much
Sometimes relationships get rushed
And you don't know what you have gotten yourself into
until after the first bubble gets bust
and then you realize the other person's shit does stink
when the toilet jams and don't flush
Like conjoined twins, I thought we would both die
if something ever came between us
We said we would be together forever
but fate didn't believe us
To me, you were my Goddess Venus, but to you,
I became like the Mark Antony statue
Just another man with a penis
You cunning, seductive, backstabbing,
selfish, stuck-up, genius
You told me you loved me a few paragraphs ago
So both to me and my readers, for chapters
you simultaneously teased and deceived us
I tried over and again to leave you,
but kept returning in stupidity like Jason sequels,
until I prayed to Jesus.

Who granted me the common sense and strength
to break the shackles
of my emotional attachment to you,
that finally freed us.

CHAPTER TWENTY

The cell phone rang at least ten times before Daunte decided to answer.

"Hello."

"How long have you been back?" Antonio asked in a low tone.

"Just got in about ten minutes ago. Look, man, we gotta talk, I got saved today and ..."

Antonio began weeping loudly over the telephone, interrupting Daunte in the middle of his testimony.

Antonio proceeded to tell Daunte what happened over the weekend with Faith. Daunte sat in silence. He knew the devil was not going to allow his soul to go to the Lord without a fight. The pastor had preached that when the devil sees that he cannot get to you because you have the Holy Spirit protecting and guiding you, he tries to throw you off your blessings by coming through those you love or associate with that haven't made God a priority in their lives. The devil's only purpose is to seek, kill, and destroy everything with which he comes in contact. Daunte was not going to allow the devil the satisfaction of destroying what

God had built for him today. So he held back his anger and forgave Antonio.

"Man, I'm sorry. I'm truly sorry," Antonio confessed, sounding contrite.

"That's really fucked up what you did, but I forgive you, dawg," Daunte said, trying to hold back his emotions.

"Dawg, she ain't shit. I told you that. She's a ho, my nigga. I tried telling you, but you didn't want to listen," Antonio said, projecting his voice a little louder.

Daunte didn't respond.

"Did you get your letter from Dr. Johnson yet?" Antonio asked.

"Yeah, I got it the day I left for New York. I'm still thanking God that it was negative. I know yours was too, right?" Daunte asked, praying that he was going to tell him yes.

Antonio started sobbing again over the receiver.

"They got me, playa."

Antonio's sniffling had muffled the sound of the spinning barrel of the .38 special that he had palmed in his hand.

"Who got you?" Daunte demanded to know.

"The bitches. They got me, nigga. After all the bullshit I ran on these hoes, it finally came home to rest," Antonio said as if he knew that one day it was going to happen.

"You're talking crazy now. Why don't you come over so we can talk?" Daunte asked, hoping he could somehow help his friend.

But Antonio was beyond being helped. All he could think about was justifying why he had slept with Faith before he made his next fatal decision.

"I got that bitch, Faith, real good for you. She let me hit it raw, my nigga. So now she has what she deserves, but I'm not going to succumb to AIDS like that ho. I control my own destiny, not a muthafuckin' disease that some dirty lil' bitch gave me. I tell you that!" Antonio said, sounding more fatalistic than afraid.

"Antonio, I hope you ain't talking about killing yourself. Also, how could you do that to Faith? I just don't understand. Antonio, if you take your own life you will be sending your soul straight to hell, and that's what the devil wants. We really need to meet up. You got me nervous," Daunte said as he made his way to his truck.

"Don't you know that we are already in hell and death just puts us in the final line of judgment? Ain't no need for you to try to be no hero, dawg. By the time that you do find me, it'll be too late. I just called to let you know that I love you and I'm sorry."

Antonio dropped his cell phone and placed the loaded .38 special into his mouth. He took a slow breath and then pulled trigger, blowing his brains out of his skull and onto the driver and passenger windows of his 2006 Maybach 57 S.

Missing You
I can't believe that you're gone,
we should have stayed close
My Blood
My love
My Guardian Angel
My Ghost
I wish before, it was more that I gave
than now frequent visits
with reminiscing conversations
and flowers at your grave
I'm angry with your earthly body
for not being strong enough
to allow your heavenly spirit to stay
I try to pass the time by writing to help ease the load
Even now as I write this, I can feel the tears explode
I tried to move on but there are
so many unanswered questions that I hold
Death came sudden and swift like a thief in the night
I prayed for your soul as your flesh was losing the fight
I screamed to death to leave you alone
but you must have got enthused with the light
Now when I see your pictures, I lyrically write scriptures
That gives me the strength to finally go on
and your memory will remain my motivational seed
that allows me to stay strong
Until my fate takes place and the Lord calls me home.

EPILOGUE

Daunte held onto Antonio's mother, Mrs. Roberts, as she broke down at the sight of her son's closed casket. Daunte thought about how much he dreaded funerals. Death didn't give you time to prepare for its arrival. It came and took without warnings and without final goodbyes. Death didn't care about closed or open caskets, or even if the lifeless corpse that it left behind had a funeral at all.

After the burial, Daunte and Antonio's parents remained at the gravesite long after everyone else had left. Mr. Roberts finally convinced Mrs. Roberts to go home with him so she could get some rest. She finally agreed when it began to rain. They advised Daunte that he should be heading home also because it was getting dark. The Roberts said their final farewells to their beloved son before departing. Daunte sat on a tree stump speaking to his fallen comrade when an eerie figure walked up. The stranger stood for a moment and stared at Daunte from the shadows before he took off his hood and revealed himself.

"Oh shit! Antonio, you got a visitor. It's our nigga, Mr. Burnt Out Pete! I'm mad that you missed the service, but I'm glad to see you here now," Daunte said as he stood up to shake Pete's hand, but his greeting went unanswered.

"Don't you ever fuckin' call me Burnt Out Pete any muthafuckin' more, do you hear me, nigga?" Pete demanded with fire in his eyes as his nostrils flared. "Do you really think I came to pay respect to this bitch-ass nigga?"

Daunte was in disbelief at what he was hearing. Before he could react, Pete continued.

"Yeah, muthafacka, I know 'bout all them 'Burnt Out Pete' jokes you and this nigga cracked. I know 'bout the story y'all muthafuckas tell about my mama burnin' me in the fuckin' oven. Pay respect? Y'all niggas talk about respect? For years y'all been disrespecting me. I always knew when the time was right that payback was going to be a bitch. Matter of fact, yo bitch, Bitch!" Pete said with confidence and authority.

"That's right, nigga, and don't try to act bad neither because I got something that will put you flat on yo skinny ass," Pete said. He then revealed a pistol that he had concealed inside his pants.

Daunte's face reddened, but he didn't speak a word as Pete told his story of revenge. Pete reminded Daunte of the night that Daunte had last paged him for a bag of weed. He went on to explain that when he called back, Faith answered, crying and upset. She told him how she was tired of being mistreated and cheated on by Daunte. Pete listened patiently and sympathetically. After an hour of talking, Pete convinced her to let him come over because his battery was dying on his cell phone and he wanted them to talk some more. His apparent purpose was to console her, but his real goal was to get into her panties before Daunte came home. Pete laughed to himself as he told Daunte how he sat in his house smoking with his woman. He also threw wood on the fire by vilifying Daunte, telling Faith that he was still fucking some of the same hoes that he had met before her.

Faith called Pete the next day, telling him that Daunte had found the rest of the weed that they had left. She believed Daunte's stupidity had caused him to fail to realize that he didn't have any more weed before he left and that was the main reason that he had paged Pete last night in the first place. So Daunte had smoked the remaining hydro that Faith and Pete shared on the couch together. As Daunte listened, he thought of reaching for Pete's gun, but his eyes must have given away his plan. Pete grabbed the handle of his gun and gave Daunte a pleading look to go for it. After Pete got his point across, he continued with his story.

Pete went on to tell Daunte how he tried to fuck Faith that night, but she was bullshitting. He commented that if he were a faggot lookin' muthafucka, he probably would've got some ass that night. Pete explained that his time did come, though. Faith called him one night, after Antonio had left from paying her a short visit. Little Dick Willie had opened the doors for Pete to swing his eleven-inch python on her. Pete bragged on how he had fucked Faith without a rubber and how good she sounded when she screamed. Daunte clutched his fist. Pete, seeing that Daunte was incensed, mocked his movement with laughter.

Daunte thought to himself that he had to make a move. He wasn't the type of nigga who could sit back and play the bitch role. Growing up in the D as a pretty boy, he had to show muthafuckas too many times that he wasn't a ho. So he was ready to scrap with a nigga at any time.

His grandma told him a long time ago, "If you don't stand for something, you will fall for anything." Daunte's plan was to hit this nigga as hard as he could and either try to run or stomp his ass to death.

Then Daunte got to thinking: this was Pete. Daunte wasn't going to kill, or be killed, over no muthafuckin' female or anyone else. It was cool if Pete wanted to end the friendship. Fuck him. Pete had always been a jealous muthafucka anyway. Let him and Faith have each other. Besides, when Tony slept with Faith without a condom, it sealed Faith and Pete's inevitable fate. Daunte accepted the betrayal and was ready to move on. The Lord had already spared him from the incurable disease of death that his modern day Judas friend was now cursed with. He had another chance at life and wasn't going to let it pass him by fighting or dying over a female. The Geto Boys's song "Let a Ho be a Ho" couldn't be any truer at that moment.

Fuck this, I'm going home, he concluded to himself as he turned and walked away from Pete's mumbled warnings. Daunte said goodbye to Antonio as he headed back to his car.

"Bitch, don't turn your back on me!" Pete turned his mumbling words into a direct command.

"Faith tried turning her back on me. She told me that she was going to the funeral to see how you were. She wanted to tell you that she was sorry and she didn't mean to hurt you. After all the shit I did for her, I couldn't let that shit happen. You don't deserve a woman like Faith. I told her she couldn't go, and do you think she listened to me? I told her not to turn her back on me, but she did it anyway." Pete choked up as he spoke.

"So I grabbed her by her neck, just so she could stay still for a second, but she started punching and kicking. She didn't stop. I told her to, but again she didn't listen. I thought she musta come to her senses because her punches had turned into taps and her taps stopped soon after. I thought she had finally given in. I thought we were going to be able to sit and talk, but when I let her neck go, she just dropped. I tried to wake her, but I couldn't."

Daunte stared at Pete with enmity in his eyes.

"What are you looking at? You the reason she's dead. You had to have them all, didn't you? Why couldn't I have somebody like Faith to love me?" Pete yelled as he wiped the tears from his eyes with the side of his firearm.

Daunte didn't say a word. He turned around and said his goodbyes again to Antonio and proceeded to walk away.

"Didn't I tell you, muthafucka, not to turn your back on me?"

Pete lifted his gun and aimed it in Daunte's direction. The first shot whistled over Daunte's head, missing its target, and made its new home in an old oak tree. Daunte was unlucky when the second bullet fired and pounded into his back. Daunte's legs gave out and he fell in a slant motion like a timber tree being chopped down. His whole body became debilitated as his blood mixed with the mud. He tried to move, but his legs felt like they were stuck in dried cement.

Daunte's life flashed before him. He thought about the game of *Time Out* that he and Antonio had played during the majority of their youth. Today he was flicked a *Time Out* card and it had a new meaning. This one was permanent. There was no coming back from it. There wouldn't be any plans of getting married and having children for him.

Daunte thought about how bad his mama was going to take his death. She had always worried too much, especially when it came to her kids. She would always tell him to be careful when he went out and to always remember to watch his back. She told him: "Everyone you think is your friend is not your friend. There are a lot of people out there who act like they are, but they really don't like you. That's why, son, you have to be careful who you associate with and call your friend."

Daunte would always tell his mama, "I know ma. I love you, but I know how to take care of myself. Please stop worrying. I will be OK."

Now he wished he had taken her warnings more seriously. He also thought of his brothers and sisters. He wished he could have spent more time with them, instead of chasing females around all day. He thought of Dot and how lonely she would be. She didn't have too many female or male friends, so she had looked forward to the times that he would come over to chat with her. He would miss her. She was the only true female friend he had. The rest were just girls who wanted to be with him. He imagined himself bringing his future wife to meet her and they would all laugh about the trials and tribulations he went through to find true love.

Daunte's thoughts were quickly interrupted by Pete's splashing footsteps closing in fast. Daunte's desire to live gave him the strength to lift his head momentarily. As his eyes searched for freedom, Pete hovered over him like the Grim Reaper. He aimed and then shot Daunte at point blank range in the face, freeing his spirit from his paraplegic body that doubled as his death trap. Pete bent down and poked him with the nose of the .357 Magnum, making sure that Daunte was dead. Headlights flickered from the darkened cemetery road before the waiting getaway vehicle pulled up to the curb of the murder scene. Pete hopped in and he and his accomplice sped off into the black rain. As Pete made his escape, he stared at the corpse of his childhood friend that he envied even in death.

"Do you think we'll regret messing with so many females?" Daunte had once asked Antonio.

"Probably not until the day we die," Tony had replied.

Daunte's Last Words

My life
My death
So much time wasted, now none is left
As my vessel awaits for my assassin to commit murder
why don't God help?
My flesh is getting cold and all my mind
can do is flashback
on my adolescence while my adrenaline rushes
and tries its best to hold and keep alive my soul
I know this gotta be a dream is what I screamed
as my spirit was released from my body
by the murderous slug
from the pretend to be thug
Who decided to end my life because
"He just wanted to be loved"
I closed my eyes as I floated with the wind
Lord I pray: Please father forgive me for my sins
Is this how my last chapter unfolds?
If so, I wish I could have had my story told slow
I tried to hold on as long as I could, but the voices
kept telling me to let go
As death approached, he wasn't going to allow me
to deny their request
So this last verse that you're reading
is also the last of my breath.

Wake-up Call

Forty million people worldwide are living with HIV/AIDS.

In 2002, HIV/AIDS was among the top 3 causes of death for African American men aged 25–54 years and among the top 4 causes of death for African American women aged 25–54 years.

In 2002, HIV/AIDS was the number one cause of death for African American women ages 25- 34.

Even though African Americans account for less than a quarter (13%) of the US population, they account for about half (50%) of the people who get HIV and AIDS.

The rate of AIDS diagnoses for African American adults and adolescents was 10 times the rate for whites and almost 3 times the rate for Hispanics. The rate of AIDS diagnoses for African American women was 23 times the rate for white women. The rate of AIDS diagnoses for African American men was 8 times the rate for white men.

During 2001–2004, African American men, a term that includes adults and adolescents, accounted for 44% of HIV/AIDS diagnoses in men in the 33 states with long-term, confidential name-based HIV reporting.

In 2004, more African American children (under the age of 13) were living with AIDS than were children of all other races and ethnicities living with AIDS combined

Source:
Centers for Disease Control
http://www.cdc.gov/hiv/

LOOK FOR MORE HOT TITLES FROM

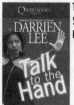

TALK TO THE HAND – OCTOBER 2006
$14.95
ISBN 0977624765

Nedra Harris, a twenty-three year old business executive, has experienced her share of heartache in her quest to find a soul mate. Just when she's about to give up on love, she runs into Simeon Mathews, a gentleman she met in college years earlier. She remembers his warm smile and charming nature, but soon finds out that Simeon possesses a dark side that will eventually make her life a living hell.

SOMEONE ELSE'S PUDDIN' – DECEMBER 2006
$14.95
ISBN 0977624706

While hairstylist Melody Pullman has no problem keeping clients in her chair, she can't keep her bills paid once her crack-addicted husband Big Steve steps through a revolving door leading in and out of prison. She soon finds what seems to be a sexual and financial solution when she becomes involved with her long-time client's husband, Larry.

THE AFTERMATH
$14.95
ISBN 0977624749

If you thought having a threesome could wreak havoc on a relationship, Monica from My Woman His Wife is back to show you why even the mere thought of a ménage a trios with your spouse and an outsider should never enter your imagination.

THE LAST TEMPTATION – APRIL 2007
$6.99
ISBN 0977733599

The Last Temptation is a multi-layered joy ride through explorations of relationships with Traci Johnson leading the way. She has found the new man of her dreams, the handsome and charming Jordan Styles, and they are anxious to move their relationship to the next level. But unbeknownst to Jordan, someone else is planning Traci's next move: her irresistible ex-boyfriend, Solomon Jackson, who thugged his way back into her heart.

LOOK FOR MORE HOT TITLES FROM

Q-BORO
BOOKS

DOGISM
$6.99
ISBN 0977733505

Lance Thomas is a sexy, young black male who has it all; a high paying blue collar career, a home in Queens, New York, two cars, a son, and a beautiful wife. However, after getting married at a very young age he realizes that he is afflicted with DOGISM, a distorted sexuality that causes men to stray and be unfaithful in their relationships with women.

POISON IVY – NOVEMBER 2006
$14.95
ISBN 0977733521

Ivy Davidson's life has been filled with sorrow. Her father was brutally murdered and she was forced to watch, she faced years of abuse at the hands of those she trusted, and was forced to live apart from the only source of love that she has ever known. Now Ivy stands alone at the crossroads of life staring into the eyes of the man that holds her final choice of life or death in his hands.

HOLY HUSTLER – FEBRUARY 2007
$14.95
ISBN 0977733556

Reverend Ethan Ezekiel Goodlove the Third and his three sons are known for spreading more than just the gospel. The sanctified drama of the Goodloves promises to make us all scream "Hallelujah!"

HAPPILY NEVER AFTER – JANUARY 2007
$14.95
ISBN 1933967005

To Family and friends, Dorothy and David Leonard's marriage appears to be one made in heaven. While David is one of Houston's most prominent physicians, Dorothy is a loving and carefree housewife. It seems as if life couldn't be more fabulous for this couple who appear to have it all: wealth, social status, and a loving union. However, looks can be deceiving. What really happens behind closed doors and when the flawless veneer begins to crack?

Q-BORO
BOOKS

WINTER 2006

PREVIEW
Someone Else's Puddin'
By Samuel L. Hair

Coming in December 2006 from Q-Boro Books

Prologue

When Melody entered room 222, Larry was lying naked across the bed, erect as penitentiary steel, and smoking a joint of chronic. She wasted no time getting naked and pouring herself a glass of vodka. As Larry relaxed, entertained by porn movies and her 38Ds, he smiled.

"You're my baby, Melody. Believe it or not, you're the best thing that's ever happened to me. I love you and I always will, no matter what."

She enjoyed hearing those words, especially coming from Larry, and not from her ghetto-fied, institutionalized husband who couldn't seem to stay out of prison for more than two months at a time.

Larry had stuffed his paraplegic wife, Pat, with tranquilizers, assuring she would remain asleep while he snuck out for his rendezvous with her beautician, Melody. Meanwhile, Melody had filled her teenage son's request for McDonald's and Taco Bell. Afterward, while watching BET, her son fell asleep. The secret lovers both had green lights. Luckily, the rich and ruthless Michelle, Melody's extremely jealous lesbian lover, had no knowledge of Melody's date with Larry. This was a good thing, since Michelle was known to kill when it came to someone messing around with her puddin'.

Larry had rented a suite at the Travelodge for the entire month—a luxury hideaway for himself and Melody to get away from life's issues, problems, and also from people who knew them and their spouses. It was a six-day-a-week ritual for the secret lovers to meet between two and six p.m. to socialize, have a couple drinks, and to have uncut, explicit sex.

They made each other feel needed and appreciated. Unfortunately, on this particular day, their date was delayed due to Pat's illness.

The fact that they were both married didn't matter to them. They had grown accustomed to fooling around with someone else's puddin'. They had kept their relationship a secret for over four years, and not once had Melody thought of saying no to Larry, dismissing him, or rejecting him for any reason, not even for her mother, who had advised her several times to break off her relationship with the married man. After all, he was the man who showered her with diamonds, gold, a variety of other expensive gifts, paid her house note, car note, dressed her son in name-brand tennis shoes and designer clothing, and gave her raw, pleasurable, uninhibited sex. Under no circumstances was she going to dismiss him out of her life. No way in hell.

After taking another long swallow of Popov vodka, she began showing her appreciation for all the things he had done for her. She fell to her knees like she was about to pray, while he sat comfortably at the edge of the bed sipping vodka. She then took his long, fat penis into her hands and began gently massaging and stroking it. Then she began sucking, licking, and slurping in exactly the way he had taught her.

"Uumhmm, yes, baby, yes. Damn, you make me feel so good," Larry moaned. Gradually, she sped up her rhythm, causing him to quiver and tremble, which is something his wife had never done. She thought about bringing him to a climax, but quickly dismissed the thought.

"No, baby, not now. I want to feel your hot, thick juice inside me," Melody said.

She brought her lips and tongue to a halt and quickly exchanged positions with him. It was now her turn. He ran his snake-like tongue up and down her legs while twirling three long, fat fingers in and out of her hot, juicy womb. He then began licking her clitoris, causing her to move rhythmically and have tremors that triggered breathtaking multiple orgasms. They had been sexing one another for so long that they had mastered each other's bodies and knew when the other was about to climax.

"I want it, baby. Now." Melody moaned, giving him the signal to immediately enter her. Suddenly he flipped her like a pancake, and she dutifully bent over and grabbed the edge of the bed. Impatiently, he thrust his rock hard penis inside her hot, wet, trembling tunnel of passion. His strokes were slow and deep and his penis touched all the right spots.

"Ooh, yes, give it to me, Big Daddy. Yes, damn, I want it all," Melody begged. At that moment he pulled out, flipped her on her back as if he was angry, and she instinctively placed her legs over his shoulders. He thrust his hard, throbbing penis inside her, plunging into the depths of her womb, riding her with rough passion, pounding like a jackhammer, just the way she enjoyed it. Her cries of pleasure filled the room and caused a crazed, wild look to develop in his eyes. He plunged harder, deeper, and faster, and then suddenly, simultaneously, they exploded like volcanoes in full eruption. Afterward, they lay side by side totally spent, but relieved of all stress and daily pressures.

Mission accomplished. And so they returned to their spouses.

FLIP BOOK NOW TO READ

DETROIT
SLIM

DETROIT SLIM

A multi-ending urban tale
by
Geavonnie Frazier

Never leave an enemy behind you, so that he might rise up and
strike you from behind.

The Heist

"Who is it?"

"It's Doobaby! Man, I need to get on the crap table so I can win back some of my money. If I don't, my old bird gonna kill me!"

"Yeah! Yeah! Yeah! If you keep banging on that door like you crazy, then yo' mama gon' be the least of your problems," the stocky doorman replied as he closed the peephole of the Hole in the Wall, an after hours club.

In a slow motion movement that mimicked *The Matrix*, he unlocked the dead bolt and removed the chain from the door that kept death waiting impatiently. The doorman opened the door to see Doobaby standing before him with an unsatisfied hunger in his eyes. Five men dressed in all black stood behind the savage, with eyes as cold as the devil.

As an ex-police officer turned bouncer, the doorman's mind started to warm up to the signals of danger that faced him. First, the lookout kid had called off that night because he suddenly got the flu. Then Jason, the outside guard, took his lunch break early and went in the opposite direction of his usual spot, Sammy's Chili Bowl. The doorman recalled watching Jason as he walked off, and every two seconds he would turn around to see if the doorman was still watching. When he made it to the corner, instead of making a left in Sammy's direction, he made a right and gave the doorman a daunting look as he disappeared around the corner.

To the doorman, it must have seemed liked a moment frozen in time, but the clock was ticking quickly on the watches of his soon to be assailants.

Suddenly, Doobaby was shoved to the side by one of the men in black. The man pulled out a sawed-off shotgun that was concealed in his unfastened overcoat. The doorman awoke from his daze and tried frantically to close the door, but unfortunately the shotgun shells hit the ground before he came completely out of his trance. The gang put on their ski masks and stormed into the club. As the robbers got into position, Doobaby made his exit. There were five armed men who entered through the front, and three others were at the back, waiting to get in.

He-Man, the strong-arm better known as The Punisher, was the leader of the criminal operation that night. He was also an officer on the Detroit Police Force. He-Man demanded full cooperation or otherwise everyone in the club would be killed, without hesitation.

Butter was in charge of gun retrieval. Everyone had to check their guns. Clifford was the lookout guy. He manned Frankie the Maniac's police radio and would notify them if the cops were coming.

Black Sam acted as the doorman, replacing the one who was dead at his feet. If anyone came to the door during the holdup, he would deny them entry. For the persistent ones, he would inform them that they had undercover cops in there, casing the joint. He knew that would be enough to scare off the biggest gambler. They would rather lose their rent money than spend one night in jail.

Bobby and Jimmy Jackson, a.k.a. Big Twin and Little Twin, were the eyes and ears of the operation. They watched everyone and listened for everything, especially the ones who looked like they wanted to make a run for it. The sight of a bullet catching a hostage in the head made the patrons take their unwanted guests seriously.

Frankie the Maniac, also an officer of the Detroit Police Department, and Damon the Devil, a local neighborhood bully, worked closely together. They were in charge of collecting everyone's money and valuables. They bagged everything from minks, to bezeled fronts, to all the cash they could pack into the duffle bags, including the bartender's tip cup.

The gang stole as much as they could before they decided to close shop. Butter drove the Expedition expertly as he backed it up to the shipping door so it could be loaded with the stolen loot and jewelry.

"All right, people, the worst is over. Don't make this any more complicated then what it has to be. So far I only count two dead and that's a good thing because we planned on killing all you muthafuckas," Frankie said as he walked backward toward the exit with his gun held high.

"You all are dead men. This is Slim's joint, nigga! What you did here tonight will be nothing compared to what Slim is going do to your asses," an old man said and laughed.

That statement didn't sit well in He-Man's stomach, but he couldn't allow his crew to see it, so he reacted like every coward who tries to lead a gang of weak followers. He walked back in, aimed his gage at the old man's face, and without a word, pulled the trigger. The old man's face splattered like a busted watermelon as the rest of his body staggered without its commanding post.

"Anyone else got something to say?" He-Man asked as all gasps and whispers stopped. The only sound that could be heard was the hard thump of the old man's body hitting the floor as He-Man walked out of the club calmly watching everyone with a hawk's eye.

They sped away to the hideout, which was an abandoned house on the east side of town. They unloaded the trucks and then the twins drove off to ditch them in the Detroit River. The rest of the gang stayed at the house to help count the profits from the heist.

"We got over a million in cash and about three hundred thousand in jewelry and furs. Dawg, we did it! We did it big!" Clifford exclaimed.

"Calm your ass down. You're the type that will go out and start running your mouth and get us all busted. Nobody say shit. Ya heard me?" He-Man shouted as a couple of men from the group agreed.

"That's right, that's right."

A hard knock on the door startled the men. Frankie and He-Man moved into position with infrared lights from the carbine aimed at the door.

"Who is it?" Black Sam asked through the cardboard window of the HUD house.

"It's Jason and Doobaby," the security guard answered.

"Let them in," He-Man commanded.

Black Sam opened the door with a snub-nosed .38 pistol pointed in the face of their visitors.

"Fellas, is there a problem? Didn't I tell you to lay low for a while until this shit cool down?" He-Man asked with such wickedness that the men were afraid to answer.

"That was Slim's club, man! I didn't know that Slim owned that spot. I heard that nigga is really pissed off! I heard one time that his best friend stole from him, so he cut off all his fingers to show his crew that he no longer had a right hand man!" Doobaby shouted until his fragile body was exasperated.

The rest of the gang stood terrified at the news because everyone had heard at least one story in their life about the madman, Slim.

Detroit Slim

Raymond Daring, a.k.a. Slim, was born on June 19, 1963. That was the same day his mother abandoned him on the doorstep of Salomon's Catholic Church on Detroit's west side. During his childhood, Raymond went from one foster home to the next. People were afraid of him because he didn't talk much and seemed a little weird, so no family ever wanted to adopt him. He got his first nickname Junebug, because every time his birthday came around, he would bug everyone he knew for a gift.

By the age of seventeen, he got a job working for a Polish immigrant by the name of Paul Jarosinski. Mr. Jarosinski owned a small deli in Hamtramck, a little town inside the city of Detroit. Junebug worked from open to close because he had gotten kicked out of the foster home he was living in for smoking weed, and he didn't want to go back to the orphanage. Junebug often came to work early to get inside from Michigan's freezing winter weather. He was such a hard worker that Mr. Jarosinski allowed him to sleep in the deli after the place was closed. Junebug was the only black person who lived in the all Polish-American neighborhood. Sometimes these two teenage Polish kids would come by and yell obscenities to him as he tried to sleep.

"Hey, wake up, you ugly fucking nigger!" one boy yelled.

"Yeah, nigger, why are you in our neighborhood? Why don't you go find a Kentucky Fried Chicken in the ghetto to work at? I'm sure if you're a good boy, they'll pay you with some fried chicken and pinto beans." The young boys laughed.

One night Junebug filled his sleeping bag with sheets and pillows to make it appear as if he was still in it. The boys came by yelling again as they usually did, calling him everything but a

child of God. Junebug came from around the bushes with a Louisville slugger baseball bat and started swinging it wildly. He beat the boys so badly that they begged and pleaded for him to stop. Word spread quickly that the black guy that worked at A Little Taste of Poland was crazy.

One day, a group of well-dressed Polish gangsters came into Mr. Jarosinski's deli while they were closing. Junebug was trying to lock the door when they barged in.

"Hey, Paulie, why the fuck haven't you been paying your protection money on time lately? What's the fucking deal with that?" one of the slick-haired men asked.

"Fuck off," Paul said as he stopped sweeping and grabbed his crotch.

"Look at this, Joe, this fucking loud mouth is showing off in front of the nigger," another man responded.

Junebug pulled out a little black six-shot revolver and aimed it straight at the man's head. Everyone in the room was shocked and didn't move quick enough to draw their weapons.

"Junebug, put that gun down!" Mr. Jarosinski yelled.

"Mr. Jarosinski, I ain't gonna let no one fuck wit' you. You've been like a father to me," Junebug said as he cocked back the pistol.

"Listen, Slim, you don't want to do that shit. Nobody is going to fuck with Paulie. He's my big brother. We were just pulling his chain. Now put the fucking gun down!" Joe requested.

Junebug looked over to Paul and he shook his head in agreement. Junebug lowered his gun, but it remained cocked.

"Jesus! Paulie, what kind of maniac you got working for you?" Joe asked as he and the rest of the boys laughed.

Paul hugged and shook hands with the men.

"Junebug, this is my little brother, Joey Jarosinski. That is our cousin, Vincent, better known as Handsome Vinnie, and this is our other cousin, Rick Nowak, better known as No Lips Ricky. They call him No Lips because when this fucking guy talks, his lips never fucking move. In his past life he must have been a fucking ventriloquist," Mr. Jarosinski joked as the men joined in on his laughter.

"You got some kind of balls, kid, pulling a gun out on us like that. You could have been killed," Ricky stated.

"You fucking pricks were too slow to react. Shit, if this kid was a sharpshooter, we all could've been dead." Joe sarcastically laughed at his crew's incompetence.

"We need someone with balls and quickness like yours. We need someone like you to work for us," Joe continued. "And we'll pay you a lot more than working in this fucking deli. So what do you say, Slim?" Joe asked.

"Why do you keep calling him Slim? His name is fucking Junebug," Paul commented.

"Junebug? He look like a Slim to me. Now that's a fucking name. Where you from, Slim?" Joe asked.

"Detroit," Slim proudly answered.

"There you have it. His new fucking name is Detroit Slim—the killer."

Slim began working for the Jarosinski crew immediately. They had him doing nickel and dime gigs until they could trust him. After a couple of months passed, he was put in charge of collecting protection money from local businesses. Their operation had spread from Hamtramck to Ann Arbor in just a few months. Slim started reading books on organized crime and old century torture methods. He was fascinated with knife and dagger tortures. He learned 229 ways to torture and kill a man

with a single blade. His love of reading kept him from being careless like others before him. He studied law and paid close attention to the stories of successful gangsters who had everything, but lost it all. Slim became a notorious hit man for the crew, and a loyal leader to those who followed him. His entourage of criminals grew quickly as men flocked from everywhere to work for the rising kingpin.

Doing work for the Jarosinskis was getting too small for Slim's appetite. He wanted to take over Detroit, but Joe Jarosinski would not give him the go-ahead. Slim wanted to get rid of Joe, but his respect for Paul had spared Joe's life. After Handsome Vinnie and a couple of Arabs got busted for selling kilos of cocaine to undercover cops, No Lips Ricky and Joe began feuding over who controlled Vinnie's turf. Ricky believed Joe was making careless mistakes and decisions, so he and some of the other boys began to question Joe's ability to run the family-based organization. Slim decided to play on the rivalry between the two by keeping the tension tight. When Paul became sick, Slim knew that Joe's time to live would come to an end soon. On his deathbed, Paul asked Slim to promise to protect Joe.

"Look after him for me, Raymond. He's my kid brother. Take care of him as I took care of you when you came to me. I know that Ricky will try to take him out after I'm gone. You have to stop this. I know he promised to give you some territory in Detroit and he would take everything else. Grant me this dying wish. I've never asked you for anything before. Can you promise me this?" Paul asked as he held Slim's hand to his lips.

"I promise," Slim answered.

Tears fell from Paul's eyes as he thanked the young boy that he often thought of like his own son. Three days day later, Paul passed away. Paul's funeral was so packed that the police

had to close off six blocks. People came from all over the world to pay their respects to the Polish immigrant who came to America fifty years before with just one dollar in his pocket. Joe and Slim had a meeting at the deli right after Paul's funeral to discuss the future of the business.

"I think we should expand our Ecstasy operation to Windsor. I have some connections that can smuggle about one hundred thousand pills by truck every month across the border. That would bring us an additional ten million a month. What do you think about that?" Joe asked.

"What do I think about that? What do I think about you making ten million more to your operation? I'll tell you what the fuck I think. I don't care how much you would make with that bullshit. I just want what is coming to me," Slim advised Joe as he smoked on his cigar.

"What are you talking about? What the fuck do you think that you should have coming to you?"

"Detroit. Do you know what else, faggot-ass Joe? I'm going to fuckin' get it."

No Lips Ricky walked in the room carrying his 9-millimeter Beretta. Joe tried to reach for his, but Slim was quicker on the draw.

"You always were the quick one, Slim," Joe said as he released his grip from his weapon.

"Yeah, and you were always the dumb one," Slim commented as he relieved Joe of his firearm.

Ricky aimed his gun at his cousin Joe and advised Slim to leave. Slim shook his head at Joe, the cold-hearted murderer whose legs trembled as pee stained his twelve-hundred-dollar suit pants.

"Slim, I started you in this shit! Ricky wanted to have you whacked, but I gave the order to let you live. This muthafucker cannot be trusted. Do you think he will let you have Detroit? That's too much money and power for a nigger to control," Joe said, sticking his foot further in his mouth.

"Detroit will be all mine, old man. I was just waiting for Paul to pass on before I proceeded. I have over ten cops in my new organization. I have a city council member, two judges, and over three hundred young, black, ruthless men and teenagers on my payroll. I also have over nine million dollars to cover the cost of making my transition to the throne," Slim boasted as he pulled out his knife.

"What? You got nine million dollars? I didn't promise you no fucking nine million dollars. Where the fuck did you get nine million dollars from?" Ricky inquired.

"I got two million dollars in the bank, three million dollars on the streets, and right now my men are at your house stealing four million dollars from your secret vault behind the bookshelf in your master bedroom," Slim said as he slithered closer to Ricky.

"What the fuck you mean, four million dollars from my vault?" Ricky asked angrily.

Slim grabbed Ricky by the face and slit his throat from ear to ear before he could get another word out. Slim cut him so fast that Ricky didn't have a chance to change the direction in which he aimed his pistol. From the sudden impact, Ricky fired his weapon, hitting Joe in the belly before he dropped.

"Slim, please help me! I'm shot! You promised Paulie that you wouldn't let anything happen to me. He told me that you promised, Slim!"

Slim approached Joe with Ricky's blood still dripping from his blade as two of Slim's men entered the deli, carrying gasoline cans.

"You promised Paulie that you wouldn't allow anything to happen to me," Joe whined.

Slim looked deep into Joe's teary eyes.

"I lied," Slim replied.

Slim was on his way to becoming Detroit's newest and youngest kingpin, but he didn't want to rule it without a queen. He was considering letting one special lady, who went by the name Ms. Lady Bug, help him rule his new empire. She was beautiful as well as ruthless. Like Slim, she had been into drug trafficking and other illegal activities since her youth. The Bonnie and Clyde couple had been seeing each for about a year before things started going downhill. Slim loved her, but her greed for personal power wouldn't allow him to fully trust her. There was only room for one ruler of Detroit, but she thought otherwise.

When Slim met Lady Bug she was small-time, pushing only an eighth of a kilo a month, but after being around Slim, she wanted to push at least six kilos a week. When Slim refused, she became infuriated and they went without speaking for months even after she discovered that she was pregnant.

After she had her baby, she got in touch with some dudes from Miami who wanted some Detroit action. In exchange, they supplied her with what she wanted and she set them up with a couple of shops in the city. Slim learned of her betrayal from local snitches on the streets. Everyone knew that Slim's permission was needed to move that much weight in the Motor City. Slim decided to call Lady Bug instead of sending a hit squad immediately after her. He didn't want to kill her, but he would tax her and her Miami connections severely. Their talk did not

go well at all. She informed him that with the help of her Miami friends, she and her family would soon be the new rulers of the D. After she hung up on Slim, he sent hit squads to bury her out-of-town visitors. Slim knew that she would be expecting him after she found out that her connections were murdered. Slim had to come up with a plan to keep the heat off himself, because he knew that she would want revenge. He knew that she had at least a couple million in cash and drugs where she lived, so he decided to let his group of rogue police officers handle her. Slim would allow them to keep the cash as a reward for their loyalty, and the drug bust would give the officers recognition they needed to get promoted.

All of Slim's plans worked without a glitch, and for the next seventeen years, he ruled the city of dope—uncontested.

Snitch

He-Man spoke up as the fearless leader that he thought he was born to be.

"I don't give a fuck if it was the president of the United States we robbed! That nigga bleed just like us. I'm the muthafuckin' police! Me and my partner, Frankie, got a plan on how we can kill that muthafucka. We'll catch him slipping one night, pull him over, and smoke his ass for resisting arrest. We'll make a little payment to the officers who used to work for him, and it's a done deal. Ya feel me?" He-Man asked as he gave Frankie dap.

"Fuck that. I'm giving my half back to Slim. Maybe he'll cut me some slack if I just return it," Doobaby whined.

"So what happens to the rest of us? Are you going to rat us out?" Damon asked, not thinking of the danger that he could be putting Doobaby in.

"No. No," Doobaby stuttered. "I ain't gonna tell him about y'all."

The once silent room filled with laughter. Everyone knew what had to be done, and it was just sad that Doobaby did not see it coming. He should have known that after that statement that he was not going to leave there alive.

Frankie walked around Doobaby slowly, staring at him like a snake stalking its prey. Frankie then turned and looked deep into the eyes of Jason as he asked him about his thoughts on the situation. The big man spoke nervously.

"Well...um...I ain't telling nobody nothing or giving back shit. I got kids to feed, man. I've been working there for two years and these muthafuckas never gave me a raise or nothing. I got stabbed and hit upside the head with baseball bats trying to keep

order at that place. Fuck that, I'm keeping mine and I'm willing to kill anybody who try to take that away," Jason spoke up, feeling enraged at the thought of losing his keep.

"Good, then we're all in agreement." He-Man smiled as Clifford and Black Sam made a sandwich out of Doobaby.

Frankie whispered something into He-Man's ear as Doobaby struggled to breathe.

"Doobaby, now you know that we can't leave any loose ends, my brotha. I worked too hard for this. We worked too hard for this," He-Man stated with his hands gesturing toward the men who had helped him accomplish the criminal task.

"Please, He-Man, I would never rat on y'all! Please. I won't say nothin', just give me another chance!" Doobaby pleaded.

"Man, I see this as an omen. I'm able to get rid of a small problem before it grows out of control. Ain't that right, fellas?" He-Man immediately received an approval from his congregation.

He-Man lit a cigarette and smiled at everyone as if he had just lost his mind for a second and then got it right back.

"Damon, I'm going to give you the privilege of taking this snitch out." He-Man handed the sawed-off to Damon, who hesitantly accepted.

"Naw man, I ain't trying to smoke nobody, dawg. I knew people might get hurt if they tried to hurt us, but I ain't no murderer," Damon said, looking at the ground to avoid looking into He-Man's eyes as they burned into him.

"What? You betta get over that shit. You still haven't made me or the rest of the boys feel like you belong in this crew. I want you to take this nigga down to the Pontiac railroads and let him rest in peace. You got it, nigga?"

"Yeah, I got it," Damon said as his strong hands grabbed Doobaby by his neck like he was a Pit Bull and dragged him outside.

"Sam, go with him and make sure the job gets finished."

"I got you, He-Man."

"Oh, and one more thing, Sam, if it comes down to it, you put them both out of commission."

Black Sam nodded as he smacked together the .45 calibers in his over-the-shoulder gun belts.

Damon ordered Doobaby into the trunk at gunpoint. Doobaby pleaded with Damon until the closed trunk of the Cadillac muffled his cries. Black Sam snuck up on Damon from the shadows.

"He-Man sent me to keep an eye on you. He don't think you got the balls to do this, and frankly, I don't either. You ain't got what it takes to be no killa. To kill a man, you have to be heartless and fearless. You ain't fearless, is you, boy? You probably pissed on yourself when he asked you to kill this little prick. I bet Doobaby wouldn't have thought about your life if Slim pulled his butcher knife out on him. That boy woulda given us all up to save himself."

"How do you know what he would've done?" Damon demanded to know.

"Because he's a coward. He wanted to give back the money, thinking that it would spare his life. As a matter of fact, why the fuck are you questioning me, nigga? He-Man gave me the green light to smoke yo ass if you messed up. So if I was you, I would watch how the fuck you talk to me."

Damon was not afraid of killing a man if he felt his life was in immediate danger. Though Doobaby posed a threat to his existence with Slim and He-Man, he couldn't find it in himself to

kill him. Damon had decided before Sam showed up that he was going to drop Doobaby off at the Greyhound bus station. He hoped Doobaby would go somewhere far away and disappear. Now that plan could no longer be put into effect, and Damon found himself stuck in an undeniable dilemma. Damon wondered how he could help Doobaby get away with Sam on his back.

Damon the Devil

Damon McCoy, a.k.a. Damon the Devil, was adopted when he was two-years-old by Bobby and Rita McCoy. The McCoy's couldn't have children of their own, so they decided to adopt. On October 19, 1987 the McCoys were watching the six o'clock news as they covered a drug raid on Detroit's northwest side. Deborah Fuller, 19, and her two brothers, Mario, 25, and Rudy, 32, were gun downed by Detroit Narcotics' officers when the Fullers open fired on the officer who tried to serve them a warrant. After the blood bath, the police found a one-month-old child under the bed. The newborn was crying while holding onto a teddy bear that had a bullet lodged in its head.

Later, the Bobby and Rita learned that Damon was the name of this infant they sought to adopt. They fought long and hard to adopt Damon. They had to allow time to pass to see if the child's biological father or relatives would show up to claim him, but no one ever did.

As a child, Damon was quick-tempered. He seemed to receive joy from making others unhappy. While other children were building tree houses, he would sit in his room plotting on the best way to cut them down. Damon received his nickname Damon the Devil from his old neighborhood because he was always in trouble. His grades were average as a child and they didn't get any better in high school. As he grew from a boy to a young man, the McCoys had their worries. They didn't know too much about his parents except that his mother and her siblings were notorious drug dealers. The mystery about his father brought on more worries about Damon's unforeseen future.

Damon didn't start making friends until the ninth grade, when he met his best friend, Duane Price, a.k.a. Doobaby.

Doobaby was two years older than Damon, but Damon's dominant personality made him look at Doobaby like a little brother. The McCoys were excited that Damon was finally making friends. Doobaby introduced Damon to rest of the neighborhood kids who were usually afraid to speak to him. After the introduction, most of the neighborhood quickly took to his following.

Damon was gigantic, not in body fat, but with muscles. He worked out just as much as most people brushed their teeth. Damon's strength and temper at such a young age often intimidated and frightened those around him, including adults. Their fear gave him power and respect, which made him yearn for more.

By the time Damon was in the tenth grade, Bobby and Rita McCoy had divorced. Bobby had left his wife of twenty-five years to be with a nineteen-year-old who interned at his job the year before. Rita was devastated by the sudden separation and had a nervous breakdown. She was never the same after she came back from her four-month stay at the Henry Ford Mental Institution. She could no longer work, so her sister Donna took her downtown and signed her up for social security. Things had become so tight that she could no longer afford to pay the mortgage each month. Mr. McCoy started coming by once a week to see how his ex-wife was doing. It hurt him to see his first love in the helpless state she was in. He never expected for her to take his leaving so badly. Mr. McCoy sold the house and put Rita and Damon into a small apartment not too far from where they used to live. He paid off the rent for the entire twenty-month lease and disappeared.

The Mission

Damon drove nervously through the midnight traffic. He couldn't think. The sound of Doobaby beating on the trunk as he begged for mercy had penetrated through the steel emotions that the 'hood had forced him to develop. Damon could see Sam staring at him out of the corner of his eye. Sam's eyes were stone cold and emotionless. His face was as black as the undying night. Damon wondered if he would even live to see daybreak. Sam's skin was so tight over his lanky frame that his skeleton appeared to be stretching through it. All he needed was a black cloak and scythe to reveal to the world that he was the Grim Reaper himself.

Sam brought Damon out his daydream and into another nightmare as he advised him that the state police were following behind them. Damon's heart pounded rapidly as sweat dropped down his brow.

"Nigga, take it easy. Just relax and drive straight. Your plates are good, right?" Sam asked calmly as though he had been in tighter situations before.

"Yeah, they're good," Damon said as he relaxed.

"Help me! Somebody help me!" Doobaby screamed as he punched the inside of the trunk.

Lights flickered and flashed as the sirens roared from the pursuing police vehicle.

Sam had sarcastically joked earlier about Damon pissing his pants, but with this development, Damon realized that it might not be as farfetched as he thought.

"Oh shit, what should we do?" Damon cried.

"We lose those muthafuckas. Put the pedal to the metal and let's get the hell out of here!" Sam shouted.

If Damon should pull over, go to the next page.
If you think Damon should pull off, go to Page 28.

Damon started thinking to himself that it could just be a routine traffic stop. If they could get Doobaby to shut up, then maybe they could get out of this one.

"Everything is legit on my car. If you can get Doobaby to be quiet, then we might be able to get out of this mess," Damon advised Sam.

Since the windows were tinted, Sam knew that the officers could not see him reaching into the back to open the moveable back seats to talk with Doobaby. Damon still drove the speed limit as the troopers kept flagging them to pull over.

"Doobaby, I know we were going to kill you, but you got to understand that it was just business."

"Fuck you!" Doobaby screamed, cutting Sam off.

"But look here, if you be quiet back there, I promise we will let you go and I promise to personally convince He-Man not to come looking for you. But if you do squeal and get us caught, you're going to jail and He-Man will probably kill Janice, that fine, sweet little whore of yours. Not to mention your mama, your daddy, your granddad..."

"I get the fuckin' point! How do I know you will keep your word?" Doobaby inquired with every bone in his body still shaking.

Sam took off his gun holsters, unloaded the clips, returned the guns back to the strap, and handed the guns and strap to Doobaby through the backseat.

"That should be a good enough down payment on trust," Sam stated as he placed the clips under his seat.

Doobaby sat silently for a brief moment before he agreed. Sam latched the seats back then returned to his seat and buckled himself in. Damon slowly pulled over to curb, took a deep breath, and parked.

"Driver, roll down your window and put both your hands where I can see them!" one officer commanded. Damon complied with the officer's orders and awaited further instructions.

"Without dropping your hands, show me with your left hand, the number of people that are in the vehicle with you!" The officer shouted through the megaphone.

Damon closed all the fingers on his right hand except for his index finger to indicate that there was only one.

"Don't fucking make me shoot you, cocksucker! I will tell you one more time. Without dropping your hands show me with your *left* fucking hand the number of people that are in the vehicle with you!" The officer shouted again, irritated at the driver's inability to follow his orders.

Damon's actions led the officers to believe that either he was nervous or high on some type of substance that could be altering his decision process. Police officers are overly cautious when dealing with those kinds of people because they can be unpredictable and dangerous, so one false move could cause the troopers to open fire. Damon followed the trooper's order this time without incident.

Damon could not believe this was happening. He only saw stuff like this on *Cops*. Then he began to really panic when he realized that he might not have hidden the sawed-off that he put in the backseat. He prayed that they didn't find it because it was the same gun that He-Man had used to murder the two men at the club.

"Passenger, roll down your window and put both your hands out of it so I can see them!"

Sam followed the same directions without a hitch. The officers now advised the driver to turn off the vehicle with one

hand and toss the keys out the window. Damon knew once he complied with that, there was no turning back. Trying to drive off to get away would no longer be an option.

The two troopers, one black and one white, approached the car, military style with their weapons drawn. The black officer walked over to the passenger side with his nine aimed at Sam's head. The white officer followed the same maneuver as he approached the driver's door.

"Don't even breathe wrong, you fucking monkey, or you're dead! Now get out of the car, turn around, and put your hands on the hood!" the white trooper yelled to Damon as his partner advised Sam to do the same.

The more the officers gave out orders, the more irate they became. Damon could no longer hear their screams over the sound of his own heartbeat. He didn't want to spend the rest of his life in prison for a murder he did not commit. The way the officers were talking, he wondered if he and Sam were going to get killed right there. He knew that he still had a chance to make a run for it, but he wasn't sure if he had the heart or the legs to do it.

If Damon should cooperate, go to Page 30.
If Damon should run for it, go to the next page.

Damon decided that he was not about to go to jail for a crime that he did not commit, even though he did participate in the holdup. He-Man had told him that nobody would be killed. Now Damon wondered if He-Man had set them up. He did send Damon out to kill Doobaby with the murder weapon from the heist. Did He-Man have this whole thing planned to cover his ass? Now, for no reason, they were pulled over by the state police.

Damon became even more frantic and paranoid as he thought more deeply into his conspiracy theory. Before he knew it, his legs were moving his body into a race for freedom, while his mind was boggled with confusion from his actions. The whole chase seemed unreal. It was like a dream that he once had, when he felt like he was running really fast but he was only moving in slow motion.

When the round of bullets were fired and struck him down like a ball of lightning, he quickly realized that he wasn't dreaming. Instead of waking up to his soft pillows and down comforter, he felt his hands and elbows scraping against the hard concrete as he tried to get back to his feet. Damon was unable to keep his balance as his head swarmed back and forth. Blood began to fill his nostrils as the air in his lungs was expelled. He struggled for air as his arm muscles gave out, which caused him to fall, face first, onto the ground. Damon tried to open his eyes to escape from the darkness that taunted him as cold chills ran down his stiffening body. A Good Samaritan turned him over and tried to stop his convulsions by shaking him before attempting CPR. For a brief moment he was able to open his eyes to see the blurred face of the woman who was trying desperately to save his life.

"Please hold on, help is on the way!" she pleaded, but they both knew that by the time help would arrive, it would be too late.

THE END

Damon pressed down on the accelerator, speeding through a red light and missing an oncoming car by seconds. The police cruiser stopped at the light briefly, allowing traffic to move out the way before it continued its pursuit. Damon could hear Doobaby's body rattling around in the trunk as he drove over bumps and corners.

Sirens seemed to be coming from everywhere, but there was not a squad car in sight. As soon as Damon made a right onto Greenfield Road, two unmarked police vehicles joined the chase.

"Oh shit, man, we're not going to make it!" Damon shouted as he tried his best to shake the unwanted company.

"Fuck that shit, we're gonna make it. Just keep driving, I'll take care of these muthafuckas," Sam said as he rolled down the passenger window of the baby blue Cadillac and began firing shots from the twin calibers. Like heat-seeking missiles, the bullets pounded into the Impalas, instantly setting them aflame.

"Yeah, y'all can't fuck wit me! You fuckin' bitches! Yeah! Yeah! Yeah!" Sam excitedly screamed out the window, not noticing the state trooper car that was right next to them, getting ready to fire.

The bullet exploded from the trooper's gun like a canon into Damon's door, as it ripped into his side. The gunshot wound caused him to lose control of the Caddy and he crashed into a parked car. The impact of the crash threw Sam twenty feet through the windshield and in front of another pursuing police vehicle, which split him in half.

Doobaby was rescued from the trunk unscathed and gave up the whole gang to the authorities for a lighter sentence. Damon survived his wounds, but was left a paraplegic, serving

life without the possibility of parole in the Jackson State
Correctional Facility.

THE END

Damon realized that trying to make a run for it would be
a bad mistake. Too many times he had watched the news and
heard about a black man getting gunned down by the police.
Living in the inner city, you learn quickly that police hate chases,
but niggas will run anyway. Damon decided to play it cool. As
long as they didn't search the car, they should be OK. Right now,
they didn't have probable cause to check the car.

The officers questioned Damon. They wanted to know
why he hadn't pulled over right away. Damon told them that he
wanted to pull over in a well-lit area because he was afraid of the
police ever since the Malice Green incident a few years ago. He
informed them that he was not trying to flee, which was why he
maintained the speed limit until he could pull over.

The officers searched the men and only came up with a
blunt wrapper in Sam's pocket.

"Do you have any weapons or narcotics in the car?" the
black officer asked.

"No, sir," Damon responded.

"What about you, boy?" the white officer asked Sam.

"Nope," Sam said, looking dead into the officer's eyes.

"What, I don't get a 'sir,' boy? Learn some respect like
your friend over here," the white officer said, stepping up to
Sam's face as his fat cheeks turned rosy red.

Sam laughed to himself. He couldn't believe this yellow-
bellied redneck was yelling and spitting all in his face. For a
second, he thought about reaching for the trooper's gun so he
could make this honky squeal like a dying pig before he split him
in half and smoked him like bacon.

"You eyeballing me, boy? You're a tough nigger, huh?"
the officer asked, ignoring the stares from his partner.

Sam decided this time not to press any more of the officer's buttons, but it was too late. The fuse was lit. The white officer advised his partner to handcuff the two while he ran their identification. Sam and Damon sat silently on the curb for about twenty minutes as they waited for the trooper to return.

"Well, Mr. Fuller, it appears that your license is in order. I pulled you over because you violated Michigan statute 257.709, which states that a person shall not drive a vehicle where a rear window or side window to the rear of the driver is composed of, covered by, or treated with a material that creates a total solar reflectance of 35 percent or more in the visible light range."

"What?" Damon asked, puzzled.

"Your tint is too fucking dark. Here's a ticket for three hundred dollars, and you have thirty days to get the tint to statute regulations. You understand, boy?" the white officer asked as he ripped off the ticket and handed it to his partner.

"Yes...sir," Damon answered uneasily. He knew he should be happy for receiving a ticket instead of jail time, but he couldn't shake off the thought of paying three hundred dollars for a bullshit-ass ticket.

The black officer took off the cuffs and handed Damon his license and ticket.

"You can leave now, boy. Your friend, Mr. Samuel Banks, has a couple of outstanding warrants in Hyattsville, Maryland for battery and child abandonment. So it looks like he'll be getting on that armored bus back east." The officers laughed with each other.

The officers didn't have to tell Damon that he was free to go twice. As soon as they said they were keeping Sam, he pulled out of there like a bat out of hell. Damon pulled around the corner from the Greyhound bus station and parked.

Damon advised Doobaby that he was going to let him go and he wanted him to be easy when he released him. From the glove compartment, Damon hit a button and unlocked the trunk. Doobaby emerged, looking battered and bruised. Damon explained to him that he had to leave and that he would send him some money when he could. Doobaby agreed and boarded the 5:30 p.m. bus to Cleveland. He could lay low with relatives until he was able to return to Detroit.

Scene of the Crime

Slim walked into the Hole in the Wall, slowly examining the scene like a lead detective. Yellow tape stretched from the front door to the back alley of the club. Homicide had already wrapped up by the time Slim arrived. News reporters hovered over the scene like vultures, trying to get footage of the dead. One of Slim's lookout kids informed Slim that Jason disappeared right before the robbery occurred. Slim's face tightened as he floated through the club with his trench coat dragging behind him, making his feet seem invisible.

Slim ordered a couple of his men to gather and burn the remaining paperwork that the police had neglected to confiscate. He ordered another group to find out what the word was on the street. He also informed his men to let the ghettos know that he was going to kill whoever was responsible for the damage and deaths in his club. Slim sent another set of his men to find Jason and bring him back to the bar. So as it was commanded, his squad of killers obeyed it.

In the Game

Several months before the Hole in the Wall robbery

"Mama, you hungry?" Damon asked of the old lady who rocked herself in the broken rocking chair while staring into space.

Rita didn't respond to his inquiry. She just kept rocking and singing under her breath. Damon went into the refrigerator, searching for something for them to eat as his stomach growled. There was a box of half eaten generic frosty flakes that they had received from Focus: HOPE on the kitchen counter. Instead of having Tony the Tiger on the box, it had a black and white picture of a hand drawn house cat. Damon grabbed two bowls and filled them with The Flakes, which was the actually the name of the breakfast treat. He then grabbed the can opener and put two triangle holes into a can of PET milk. Next, Damon shook a big ghetto bag of sugar into the bowls as he poured the evaporated milk. After all his food preparations, Rita still refused to eat. Damon swallowed his bowl with one gulp as he rushed to see who was knocking on the front door.

"What up, my nigga?" Doobaby asked as the eyeball in the peephole stared back at him.

Damon opened the door and allowed his friend to enter.

"Damn, nigga, I know you be working out and shit, but I didn't know you was the spokesman for the *Got Milk?* commercials." Doobaby laughed at Damon as milk dripped from his chin.

"Nigga, whatever," Damon laughed as he wiped his mouth with his hand.

"How mama doing?" Doobaby asked as he leaned forward into the dining room to wave at her.

"I heard my auntie and her husband talking about putting her in a nursing home," Damon whispered.

"What? Where are you going to stay?"

"Aunt Donna said I could come stay with her, but her husband said I should go to Job Corp. I ain't going to no damn Job Corp and I ain't going to let them put mama in no nursing home. I'm going to quit school and get a job so I can take care of my mama."

"You ain't going to get no job that pays you enough to do that shit, unless you get a job at the plant with your dad."

"Fuck Bobby! He's the reason we're in this predicament in the first place. If I see him again, I'm liable to go upside his head."

Doobaby sat silent for a moment before he spoke.

"Hey, there's this dude named Black Sam who keeps asking me to come work for him. He said I could make up to four hundred dollars a day."

"Then what's the problem?"

"That nigga is shady as hell."

Doobaby told Damon about a sixth grader who was walking home from school kicking rocks. The boy accidentally kicked a rock too hard and it hit Sam's car. They said the little boy apologized and offered to ask his dad for some money to fix the barely visible dent. Black Sam agreed and took the little boy home. When they arrived, his father wasn't home from work yet, but his mother was in the kitchen making dinner. Rumor is that he raped the boy's mother in front of the boy before he killed them both.

The dad came home and went nuts. He drove around the neighborhood all night trying to find out information, but no one would talk. Someone said they saw him in his car weeping when the old man from down the hall tapped on his window. The old man said he saw a tall, dark-skinned man with his son and he would be able to identify him if he ever saw him again. The father thanked the man and immediately called the police. A few minutes later, a squad car pulled up to where the men were waiting. Officer Frank Norford and Lieutenant Lamar Ortiz, better known as Frankie the Maniac and He-Man, exited the vehicle.

"What seems to be the problem?" He-Man asked while shining his flashlight into the puzzled faces.

The father tried to get out the car to explain the situation, but he was advised not to move.

"We called you! My wife and eleven-year-old son were killed, and this gentleman said he can identify the man who did it!" the man screamed in disbelief at the officers' lack of concern.

"Please, excuse my partner. There have been a lot of cop shootings in this area recently. We're just being cautious," Frankie the Maniac advised.

"We need to go to the station to look at photos so we can see if we can identify this muthafucker," the father said, interrupting the officer to let him know that he was not concerned with apologies.

"That will not be necessary, sir. I have good news for you. We already have the suspect in custody," He-Man said.

Frankie smiled. "That's right. He's handcuffed to the radiator in this old warehouse off the river. We got a tip from one of our informants who saw him with your son. This time that black son of a bitch went too far. Mister, the choice is yours. You

can give this monster what he deserves and we will turn our backs, or we can take him downtown after the old man identifies him," He-Man finished.

"I don't want any part of that!" the old man said as he shook his head.

"Sir, if you identify this guy, I will not harm him. I will let the courts bring justice for my family," the father promised as he fought to keep a tear from forming.

"OK, young man. Just let the police take care of him and hopefully that animal will never again see the light of day," the elderly man said.

The men got into squad car with the officers. They drove about twenty minutes into the city, near the old warehouses by the riverfront. They followed the officers into an abandoned building, closest to the Windsor tunnel. Glass covered the inside floors of the factory, possibly from kids throwing rocks through the windows for fun. As they walked farther into the building, the old man started feeling uneasy.

"Hey, can you guys just bring him outside? I don't see too good in the dark," the old man told the officers.

"Don't worry, everything will be fine. Is that the man you saw, right there?" He-Man pointed in the direction of the tall figure that approached them. The old man's eyes exploded with fear as his eyes met with Sam's.

"Yes that's him! Oh my God, he has a gun! Please, sir, do something!" the old man pleaded as he pulled on Frankie's uniform.

Sam jogged to the old man, expressionless, and began to pound him with the handle of the chrome magnum. The father tried to come to the man's rescue, but he received blows to the back of his head from the nightsticks of the two officers.

"I heard that they beat them guys until their skulls cracked and then they torched the place," Doobaby finished telling Damon. "That's just one of the reasons why I say that nigga is shady as hell," Doobaby said, searching Damon's eyes for a response.

To hear what happened to that family was disturbing, but Damon was not going to show that it bothered him. All the good in Damon tried to warn him not to go to work for a man who could hurt a woman and child, without a conscience. To Damon, the good outweighed the bad because he needed the money to help take care of his mama, and for two thousand dollars a week, it sounded like he could do it.

**

Damon and Doobaby decided to go to work for Black Sam. Over the next two months, they made about sixteen thousand dollars each by pushing heroin.

Damon was able to hire a part-time nurse to come by and look after his mama when he was on the midnight grind. Damon also bought groceries and paid all the utility bills. He opened a savings account for his mom so he could deposit her social security checks and let them collect interest now because he paid all their bills.

Doobaby, on the other hand, spent all the money that he made gambling. He would go to The Hole in the Wall and blow about a thousand dollars a week while his family continued to struggle.

Damon thought he would get in and save some dough, and then get out, but it was not that simple. Once he started

making that kind of money, he developed a new type of lifestyle. He became used to eating filet mignon, so how could he go back to creamed corn and neck bones?

The more Damon made, the more he began to smarten up. He started investing and saving his money, while Doobaby spent his money recklessly. Doobaby spent and lost more than what he was making. Damon knew that type of shit was not going to go on unnoticed too much longer.

One day, Black Sam pulled up to the crack house in a black Aviator with smoke-tinted windows. Sam and four other men exited the truck as a pearl white Escalade with Giovanni rims pulled up right behind them. He-Man and Frankie exited the Escalade, examining the street thoroughly as they crossed it to join the others.

"Boys, boys, boys! We seem to have ourselves a little problem here," He-Man said, looking back and forth into the eyes of Damon and Doobaby.

"What kind of problem?" Doobaby asked, dumfounded.

Damon knew Doobaby's skimming was going to catch up with them, but he was still hoping there was a way to get out of it alive.

"We'll discuss that inside," Frankie ordered as Black Sam pushed Damon and Baby inside the doors of the apartment complex out of which they were selling drugs.

Big Twin and Little Twin, who had come with Black Sam, blocked the door to keep anyone from coming in or out.

"What up, Damon?" He-Man asked while sucking his top teeth.

Damon was used to putting fear in others, but now he found himself feeling afraid.

"Hey, what's up, He-Man?" Damon's voice shook as he spoke.

"You and I both know that Doobaby has been putting his hands in the cookie jar, don't we, Damon? But you didn't do or say anything to stop it. So now I'm starting to think that you were in on it as well," He-Man accused Damon and waited a response.

Damon sat there silently. He didn't know how to respond to these accusations. He couldn't tell on his friend, even if they already knew what Doobaby was doing. He also couldn't deny Doobaby's actions because then it would be like he was spitting in He-Man's face.

"Damon didn't know anything about it. I've been taking a little bit here and there to—"

He-Man abruptly cut Doobaby off. "You've been taking a little bit here and there? Butter, hand me over the paperwork," He-Man ordered of his brother-in-law, who had also arrived with Black Sam.

Butter reached into the attaché case he carried and handed He-Man a legal pad. He-Man looked over the papers angrily before he continued.

"You've been fucking me out of about ten thousand dollars a month and you've been with us for about three months now. I'm going to assume you've been taking that much since you started, so you owe me thirty thousand dollars, muthafucka, plus interest. Now, bitch, pay up!" He-Man screamed at Doobaby as he aimed his gun at Damon's head.

"Come on now, Doobaby, do something," Damon pleaded with his friend.

"He-Man, listen man. I've been going to the Hole on the Wall, checking out the joint. I've been skimming because I needed money to be in there and see how things operated. I've

played every game in there from poker to roulette to the crap table, so I know how much they be bringing in a night. Man, these niggas is making at least 25K a night!" Doobaby explained nervously.

He-Man and Frankie looked at each other. They'd heard about how much that place was making. They were going to raid it last year but whoever owned the joint had officers in their department on his payroll. The code of crooked cops is to never fuck with other the crooked cops' clientele.

"You betta not be bullshitting me, Doobaby. I knew your ass since you were little, but that will not stop me from putting a bullet in you and your homeboy's head if you fucking wit me. Do you hear me, nigga?" He-Man asked.

"I swear on my life, He-Man. I'm telling the truth!"

He-Man lowered his gun and looked at Frankie to receive the final approval.

"Aight then, it's settled. Clifford, Sam, sit down with Doobaby and get the scoop on the place. I want to know how many security guards they got and what times they make drops to the vault. I want to know all the entrances and exits. I also want to know if you can get some inside help on this shit. C'mon, let's get moving, niggas!" He-Man ordered.

He-Man was excited, because money and power were the two things he loved the most. Doing this heist would put him on top very quickly. He hoped it would make him a powerful force to be reckoned with in Detroit.

After months of surveillance and planning, their plan was ready to go into effect. Butter had located a hideout where they could go and count the money after the heist. Clifford's job was to steal two trucks, big enough to carry the money and the rest of the guys. Doobaby recruited Jason, the outside security guard,

into the plan. Jason was going to make ten thousand dollars just to take his break early. Frankie also got one of the female police dispatchers to participate. Her job was to keep the officers who protected the club running around for about half an hour while the robbery took place.

He-Man gathered all the weapons and ammo that would be used on the job. Damon was asked to drive to Cincinnati to get the crew some black ski masks and trench coats. He-Man didn't want to use any locally purchased items, so Damon had to travel out of state to get them. Big Twin and Little Twin found a couple of Arabic jewelers who would buy whatever diamonds and furs they stole. Everything was going as planned, which made He-Man worry.

On Sunday, March 14, the men dressed in all black and loaded into the vehicles. The gang arrived on scene at exactly one a.m.

"Units 136 and 215, there is a four eleven in progress at Dave's Party and Pizza on the 5000 block of Chene and Gratiot. Caller says the suspects are two armed white males wearing blue jeans and black sweatshirts. Please respond," the female officer dispatched.

"Copy that. We're on our way. Over," most of the squad cars responded.

"All right, that's our cue, fellas! Lets go!" He-Man ordered as he turned down the portable police radio.

Since the outside guard was gone, the men had the front and back exits covered in less time than expected. When Doobaby knocked on the door, Damon could have never imagined that going in there would be one of the first of many bad decisions that would forever change his life.

On the Run

Several hours after Damon dropped Doobaby off at the bus station

Before Damon could knock on the door of the hideout, Butter whistled at him from the corner of the block. Damon left the porch and walked cautiously toward him. He-Man's brother-in-law was noticeably nervous. Butter paced back and forth as he smoked a cigarette, mumbling to himself.

"What the fuck happened?" Butter asked Damon, not looking into the eyes of the huge teenager.

"We got pulled over and they took Sam to jail on some battery shit that happened back when he lived in Maryland," Damon stated as he wondered why the hideout was abandoned.

It had only been a few hours since the police arrested Sam. Damon believed Sam was not the type that the police could break easily, but he was wrong. Butter explained that when the troopers took Sam back to the station, it only took minutes for his prints to pull up in their system. His prints matched ones that were found at six different murder scenes in Detroit, including the place where that little boy and his mother were killed.

"When they told him he could be facing up to one hundred years in prison without the possibility of parole, he started snitching," Butter explained. "They offered him a deal where he would only do twenty years and then serve twenty more on parole if he gave up He-Man and the other police officers. The district attorney's office loves cases like this, especially when an election is coming up. He-Man and Frankie have already been suspended with pay until further investigation.

Now other people are getting paranoid because of this shit." Butter looked around before taking another drag of his Newport.

"What you mean?" Damon asked as the two men walked to Butter's car.

Butter took one more puff of his cigarette before he continued.

"There are a lot of cops involved in this, some with strong political connections. This shit is not small-time at all. Sam got the names of other officers that He-Man and Frankie dealt with. So a call was made to one of the guards at the precinct where Sam is being held."

Butter looked at his watch and told Damon to get in on the passenger side of his car. Butter started the car and drove off slowly.

"Right about now, that rat's feet should be dangling from his jail cell. Everybody knew that fool was suicidal," Butter sarcastically commented as he continued to drive.

"Officers at the station where he was booked said that he didn't get a chance to tell everything yet. The FBI was going to fly out tomorrow and officially interview him in the morning. But that shit will never happen. Did you take care of that situation with Doobaby?"

"Yeah, I handled that."

Damon didn't say a word, but he breathed a little easier knowing that the police no longer had anything on them. *Did this mean that their crew was above the law?* Damon wondered.

What seemed like a long road trip was only a drive around the block. Butter pulled behind Damon's car and handed him an envelope full of hundred-dollar bills.

"This is only five thousand dollars. He-Man will give you the rest when things calm down," Butter said right before the

glass from his side window shattered violently in his face. An assailant swung the tire iron again, striking Butter across the head. Another man pulled aggressively on Damon's locked door. Damon moved the gear shift into reverse and the car began rolling backward, dragging Butter's attacker with them. The second assailant fell from the sudden movement, but he was able to get back on his feet. Halfway down the street, Damon opened the passenger's door and jumped out.

The first assailant's leg twisted and broke as the car continued to roll backward. Butter's face was covered in so much blood that Damon wasn't sure if he was dead or alive.

"You're fuckin' dead! You stole from Slim and that's your death warrant," the second assailant shouted as he fired shots in Damon's direction from about a block away.

Butter's car smashed into a parked pickup truck, stopping the vehicle's backward journey. A black Aurora pulled up next to the totaled car and sprayed it with bullets.

"Hey, that other nigga is down there! Get that muthafucka!" the second assailant yelled.

The Aurora burned rubber in reverse, doing a 360. Damon's bruises numbed as his legs sprinted from death. Bullets poured from the AK-47, hitting everything but its target. Damon ran through a narrow alley while bullets sparked at his feet. As he ran deeper into the alley, there was a closed fence ahead that blocked his passage. Damon used to run track and had an incredible ability to leap. He might be able to make it over the fence. But he thought if he ran quickly enough, he could jump onto the car and run to the other side, leaving the car to crash in the opposite direction. The part of the alley where he was running was so narrow that the assailants could no longer reach

their assault rifles out the window, so he didn't have to worry about being shot in the back as he escaped, and if they survived.

As the car got closer on his heels, he knew his choices were few, and the amount of time that he had to choose was even less.

If Damon should try to get by the car, go to page 48.
If Damon should jump the fence, go to the next page.

Damon quickly came to his senses and realized that trying to jump over a moving vehicle would be insane and suicidal. His only choice was to get over the fence as fast as he could. With the car only moments away from crushing him, he jumped onto the fence and began climbing it with Spider-Man's speed. He made it over the fence ten seconds before the car smashed into the wired gate, causing the fatal crash. Damon ran without looking back as the horn blew relentlessly from the lifeless body that lay slumped on the steering wheel.

Damon ran for what seemed like forever before he made it to back to the hideout to retrieve his car. He looked around for the second assailant before he got in. As he drove, he began to analyze all the bad decisions he had made in his life. In the past, every decision that he made turned out to be a bad one, but somehow he still made it out alive. There must be someone out there watching and praying over him. The choices he had been making recently would have usually ended with terrible results. He just hoped that whoever was looking out for him kept doing so. He needed all the help that he could get to make it out of his current situation. If he could make it out alive, he promised himself that he was going to change his life. He even thought about going to the local community college so he could get a real job to help take care of his mama.

Go to Page 49.

Damon decided to take the car, head on. He had seen it done in so many action movies that he believed he could do it. Damon knew he couldn't leap over the car, but he believed that he could jump high enough to run over it. He braced himself as the car came speeding toward him, going at least sixty miles per hour. Damon stepped back, gave himself some space, and ran toward the two-ton rolling mass of metal. His legs sprung from the ground like an acrobat jumping onto a trapeze. His mind cleared of all worries as he soared in the air. Calmness settled in and overjoyed his soul like smooth jazz on a quiet summer night. He jumped so high that he floated freely past the car and into the streets. He tried to land, but was as powerless as a falling leaf in a winter windstorm as he blew farther away.

Damon flew for so long, it seemed like an eternity had passed. As he approached his destination, he could hear what sounded like a horde of people murmuring his name. In the sky there was a bright light that shined brilliantly as it awaited his arrival, just beyond the clouds. The feeling it gave was as soothing as a mother's voice to her infant child as it developed in the womb. At that moment Damon realized that he must be dead.

Whatever force seemed to be pulling him in had allowed his memory to recall his last seconds on earth. Damon recalled seeing the car as it approached. His brain was thinking jump, but his legs didn't move quick enough to obey. The Aurora smashed into him so hard that it knocked him over the fence, killing him instantly.

THE END

Big and Little Twin's bodies were found stabbed to death in front of the precinct where He-Man and Frankie worked. The suspended officers knew that it was a message from Slim. Jason, the security guard from Slim's bar, was also found dead. His body was nailed to the front door of the Hole In The Wall. Witnesses said that Slim personally nailed him there for making the mistake of leaving his post. The gang that robbed Slim was being murdered one by one.

He-Man and Frankie wanted to go after Slim, but Internal Affairs was watching them, very closely. He-Man's wife went berserk after Butter's body was found. He had so many holes in him that they had to have a closed casket funeral. Clifford was the only one left to collect from the pushers on the streets. He-Man and Frankie couldn't do it because they were being tailed. When Clifford pulled up on the block, the streets quickly emptied. Only a few dealers turned in money, and even then, the money was short.

"Nigga, what the fuck is going on?" Clifford demanded from one of the pushers.

One of the young dealers that turned in his money looked around to see if anyone was watching before he answered.

"You know what's going on, nigga. Slim's crew is taxing all your spots and niggas ain't giving up their cut to pay y'all debts. Matter of fact, there's a hit out on you and Damon for a grand. For He-Man and Frankie they're offering 10K! So instead of killing your ass when you come pulling up on the block like you think you still a big shot, niggas respectfully walk away. I heard a couple of niggas tell Slim's men that they would do the hit on you if they offered a little bit more money. They refused, though, because they said that they will more than likely kill you

themselves," the teenager said as he released the safety on the gun inside his jacket pocket.

"All debts are now paid by me," the teenager continued. "I appreciate y'all bringing me in when I needed to make some dough, but things are getting tight again. I got a newborn that I gotta take care of and one thousand dollars sounds pretty tempting. So you need to be leaving before I decide to collect on that shit. You understand what I'm saying, Clifford? You shouldn't come around here anymore, dawg, because the next time we meet, it might be our last."

"It's like that?" Clifford asked.

"Get yo bitch ass stepping before I ice your ass right now and take back my money!" the boy commanded while staring at the roll of cash that he had just handed Clifford.

Clifford arrogantly walked away to his vehicle. He started his car and threw up the finger to the little nigga. That angered the young dealer, so he decided to make good on his word. As the young boy approached Clifford's car, he stopped short in his tracks and turned quickly in the opposite direction. Clifford gripped his nickel-plated .380 as he waited for the young punk to get closer. When he didn't, Clifford became suspicious. He looked up and down the street, but saw nothing. Then he saw Slim in the rearview mirror, staring at him from the backseat. Slim raised his butcher knife and began stabbing Clifford through the back of the leather. Slim then grabbed Clifford by the back of his braids to keep him from moving as the knife shredded his spinal cord.

Later, when the police opened the door of Clifford's car, blood poured from the 2005 Lincoln. In broad daylight, he was stabbed in his back more than fifty-five times. Everyone the police questioned said they didn't see or hear anything.

Considering Clifford's record and the fact that they didn't have any witnesses or real motives, the result of his murder was ruled as just another drug deal gone bad.

***

"Hello?"

"Hey, baby."

"Damon, is that you?"

"Yeah, it's me."

"Oh my God, where have you been? I've been so worried about you!"

"It's complicated. Have you seen my mama? I've been calling, but she hasn't answered."

"Yeah, your aunt came over early and picked her up."

"You don't know if she took her to a nursing home, do you?"

"No, Damon, I talked to her when I went across the street to help her get your mom in the car. She told me that she was going to let your mom move in with her family."

"Shit, that's good news! Tonya, I miss you so much. I wish I could see you right now."

"Tell me that you are not in any trouble, Damon Anthony Fuller."

"Baby, now you know that I never get in any trouble," Damon said as they both laughed awkwardly.

"Damon, seriously. I love you. Can you please tell me what is going on?" Tonya cried.

"OK...do you remember when I told you that Doobaby had a job for us to do?"

"No...no...no please don't say you did that shit, Damon! Please, Damon, you're smarter than that," Tonya said as she wept.

Damon felt himself fighting back his own tears. He took the phone from his ear for a brief moment so she couldn't hear his whimpering.

"I know what I did was dumb, but there has to be a way for me to get out of this. I just have to figure it out. I'm tired of watching my back. Every car that's riding my ass, I think it's following me. When I stay at friends' houses, I put their garbage cans against the garage to keep someone from hiding in it. I'm ready to go home, but there are some loose ends I have to take care of first," Damon stated, exasperated.

"Damon, please be careful," Tonya pleaded, as she knew there wasn't anything else she could do for him except pray.

"Don't worry. Everything will be OK. I love you, baby," Damon tried to reassure her before he disconnected the call.

Damon had a crush on Tonya since the first day she moved across the street from him. She wasn't very fond of him because she perceived him as a bully. Mrs. McCoy and Tonya's mom had become very good friends. Eventually, Tonya and Damon also became close. Damon acted like a bully around the rest of the neighborhood kids, but he was always a gentleman around her. In class he would write her love letters like he was still in elementary school. *If you like me, check yes. If you don't like me, check no.*

Damon always opened the door for her and never swore around her. Even as they got more comfortable around each other, he would never come around her drunk or high because he knew that she hated that. Tonya was special to him. She was a 4.0-student and championship athlete. By the eleventh grade, she

had over twenty academic and basketball college scholarships that she could choose from. Tonya didn't smoke or drink. She was five feet, ten inches tall and 135 pounds with mahogany brown skin and her hair always in braids or zillions. Her body was so curvy that she could make a professional racecar driver run off the track from distraction.

Damon and Tonya's relationship was beautiful, but the only thing Damon dreaded was the fact that she wasn't having sex until she was married. Tonya knew that marriage was not in her and Damon's near future. She had too many things that she wanted to accomplish. She wanted to play in the WNBA one day or go to law school. She loved Damon, but she was unsure if he was the one that she was going to marry. She wanted a man who brought something to the table. She didn't want a drug dealer or a high school dropout. There was something about an educated man that attracted her. She had always liked Dwayne Wayne from *A Different World*, not because of his looks, but because no matter what happened in his life he always took care of his business with school. To her, Damon was a good guy who just got mixed up with a bad crowd. She tried helping him find scholarships so he could go to college after they graduated, but he would always say he would do it tomorrow. Each time he said that, it reassured her that he was not the one that God meant her to be with.

Damon heard about the murders of the twins, Jason, and Clifford from the news. He thought about going to the cops but didn't know if he could trust them. He-Man and Slim both had officers conspiring with them in the city. Damon thought about going to a suburban police station to turn himself in. Even though the police were not looking for him, it was just a matter

of time before someone else snitched. Damon was also worried that they might not believe his story and take him back to Detroit authorities. Damon knew he wouldn't survive a night in their custody. The 'hood had taught him a long time ago that the worst thing a man could do was snitch. No matter how ignorant it may sound sometimes, it was a code to die by in the 'hood. Even though his life was in danger by his own crew, he felt that he still had to abide by it.

Damon decided that he would head east for a while. He had family in Richmond, Virginia and Tonya wouldn't be that far from him because she had decided to go Hampton University in the fall. Damon recalled a quote that he once read, "Never leave an enemy behind you, so that he might rise up and strike you from behind." Damon knew he could not leave without taking care of his enemies first.

Damon began to put together a plan. Slim was out to kill him and he believed that He-Man wanted him out of the way as well. It was now time for the ultimate setup. Damon read in the newspaper last week that Handsome Vinnie had been released from prison. Damon knew there was going to be some kind of retaliation because Slim basically slaughtered Vinnie's whole family. Damon wanted to make sure that retaliation happened. Since Slim was looking for Damon, he thought if he lured him somewhere, he could have Handsome Vinnie and his crew take him out. Damon decided that he might as well kill two birds with one stone by having He-Man and Frankie ride along for the homicide. Damon almost went nuts for a second because he didn't have a weapon, but he realized that Sam's guns and clips were still in the car. So the only thing left to do was to start making some phone calls. The first call to set off his plans was made to Vincent Jarosinski.

"Your dime, my fucking time. So what the fuck do you want?" a man with a deep Polish accent answered.

"May I speak with Vincent Jarosinski, please?"

"Who the fuck is this and what business do you have with Mr. Jarosinski?"

"My name is Damon Fuller and I have some information on an old acquaintance of his by the name of Detroit Slim."

The man covered the phone and began talking to someone in the background. Damon was trying to hear what the man was saying but could not make out the words from the muffled accent.

"What's your fucking name, kid?" Handsome Vinnie asked.

"Damon. Sir, I would—"

Handsome Vinnie cut him off before he could finish.

"Listen, Damon, if this is some kind of fucking joke, I'm going to cut your balls off and shove 'em up your ass and then replace your eyeballs with them. Do you fucking understand what I'm saying?"

"Whoa, cuz, let's take it easy! That nigga, Slim, is trying to kill me because me and some of my boys robbed one of his gambling spots. I thought since me and you got the same problem, we could work together on this shit."

"Listen, kid, Vincent Jarosinski don't *have* any fucking problems. I *cause* them. If I were you, I wouldn't fucking call here anymore. Do you fucking understand now?" Handsome Vinnie asked and then hung up before Damon could respond.

Damon knew that he needed Vinnie's help, so he had to be persistent. How could he be afraid of Vinnie when he believed that the whole city was out to kill him? If everything went according to how Damon planned, he would be the only one

walking away from this ordeal alive. Damon gave it a few minutes before he hit the redial button on his cell.

"You must don't hear too well, kid, and you're not going to be fucking hearing anything ever if you call here again."

"Listen, Mr. Jarosinski, I don't mean any disrespect. I'm seventeen years old. I was born the year after you went to prison. I'm not going to lie to you. I made a terrible mistake robbing that man. I took something that didn't belong to me, but he has done the same thing to so many other people and I know for a fact that you are one of them. I was told that he was the one who had you sent to prison. The officers who busted you were on his payroll, and so was the judge. So not only did he murder your cousins, he humiliated your family's name and sent you to prison for eighteen years. Slim is trying to murder me but I'm going to get his ass first. I will do it alone if I have to, but two guns are better than one," Damon explained to Vinnie as he thought of a Plan B.

It took Vinnie five minutes before he said a word. "Yeah…I always expected that fucking prick had something to do with me getting locked up. Eighteen years for cocaine? Fucking unbelievable! Come down to the coffee shop, kid, and tell me your fucking plans on how we can catch this rat. We're going to set a trap so big that it'll snap the fucking head off of Mickey Mouse."

If Damon should *not* trust Vinnie and explain the plan on the phone, go to Page 59.
If Damon should go meet Vinnie, go to Page 62.
If Damon is over his head and should go to the cops, go to the next page.

Damon decided that enough was enough. He did not want to be involved in this anymore. He was hurting himself and the people he loved. He had never murdered anyone and he didn't want to do it now. Meeting with Handsome Vinnie would leave him with very few choices. So Damon hung up the phone without giving him an answer. Damon knew he had to move quickly because now he just might have brought a new foe into a world where his friends were few. Damon walked to the corner of Greenfield near Six Mile Road to flag down a cab. One finally stopped and took him downtown to the Thirteenth Precinct.

Damon just wanted it to be over, so he confessed everything. Since Damon didn't play a major role in the murders, the police gave him immunity for his testimony. He had thought all cops were bad, but he realized that was far from the truth. The officers he met were honest cops. They worked hard to gather evidence to help convict the vigilante cops.

He-Man and Frankie were arrested at the precinct where they worked. Their sergeant had called them in so they could return to duty, but when they entered the station they were greeted with handcuffs. As the sergeant read them their Miranda rights, the whole morning shift applauded. Similar tactics were made when Slim's entourage of police officers were arrested. They showed up to work and each one was immediately taken into custody.

Slim wasn't so easy to get. He dug himself into one of his hideouts and prepared for war. They sent the SWAT team in four times and each time, three officers were killed. Slim had the neighborhood booby trapped with wired explosives. He had so much dynamite hidden on the streets that the wrong spark would blow up the block. The police tried to evacuate the neighborhood, but Slim had snipers all around the rooftops,

making it hard to move anyone out safely. The firefight went on for three days and four nights. The local and federal officers knew they couldn't get Slim by themselves, so the U.S. military was called in. The incident was getting international coverage and the government didn't want the rest of the world to think that they could not handle a couple of street thugs.

Around three in the morning eight black hawks hovered over the houses on Steele Street on Detroit's west side. Two special-op forces from each chopper were lowered to the ground. The block's power was cut off and the forces moved in like bats in the dark. It only took them three hours to do what it took three days for local officers to try to accomplish. After the assassinations, the special-op forces flew back out in the Black Hawks, disappearing into the morning sky. At least forty bodies were found, including that of Raymond Daring, a.k.a. Slim. He was found with a steel cord wire around his neck with twelve American flags folded thirteen times and sitting on his lap, representing the twelve officers he killed.

Damon went on to summer school and graduated with his high school diploma. Damon and Tonya then got an apartment together out in Virginia. She went to Hampton, majoring in psychology, and he went to a local community college, majoring in criminal justice. His mom remained with his aunt in Detroit and he would go visit her for a few weeks each summer. After he received his associate's degree, he transferred to Howard University, where he received his bachelor's degree. Damon and Tonya got married and moved to California to start their family and careers. They now live happily together in the Golden State with two beautiful children.

THE END

"Hey, Mr. Jarosinski I think I'm being followed, so I don't think it would be a good idea if I came to meet you. I'll just let you know how it will go down while I got you on line," Damon informed him.

"What, you fucking kidding me, right? Are you fucking nuts? Far as we know, these lines could be tapped right fucking now. Listen, kid, you get your ass down here pronto, or you can forget it."

"Mr. Jarosinski, we don't have much time if this is going to work. I'm going to call one of Slim's whorehouses and let him know that I'm looking for him. I'll leave a message for him to meet me at the old Kingsway building on Oakman Boulevard. You know Slim thinks he's invincible. So he'll show, and that is when he'll realize that he is not immortal," Damon said confidently, but still not sure if his plan would work.

"What time will you tell him to be there?"

"It's three p.m. now. I'll call him at seven and tell him to meet me at midnight."

"We're on our way there now to setup, but you better show up by eight. Understand?" Handsome Vinnie advised.

"Yes, Mr. Jarosinski. Thank you."

Vinnie hung up the phone without responding and Damon moved to the next phase. Damon scrolled through his address book on his cell phone and then dialed He-Man's number.

"Yeah," the voice on the other end answered in a low whisper.

"He-Man, we got to talk," Damon said urgently.

"I know. Where are you? I'll send someone to come and pick you up," He-Man said suspiciously.

"No, I can't move around like that. Meet me at eleven thirty p.m. at the old Kingsway building."

"That place has been closed down for years. It would be too obvious," He-Man said, still sounding like he was whispering.

"What would be too obvious? Look, dawg, that's where I'll be. Either you're there, or you're not. Eleven thirty p.m.," Damon informed him again and disconnected the call, taking control.

The bait was in place. Now all that was left to do was set the trap. Damon made his call to Slim, and his men reassured Damon that Slim would be there.

Damon arrived at Kingsway around nine thirty p.m. The side door to the old department store was kicked in, so he knew someone was inside. Damon took the safety off the two-caliber gun and walked in cautiously. It looked as though Handsome Vinnie had already setup because a spotlight was mounted by the front entrance that blinded its visitors.

"Hey, Mr. Jarosinski, it's me, Damon! Mr. Jarosinski?"

"Freeze, you muthafucker! Don't move!" the FBI yelled.

After Vinnie kept telling Damon not to talk over the phone, he did it anyway. Handsome Vinnie never left his shop because he knew the FBI was listening. So now on top of robbery and possible manslaughter charges, Damon was now facing conspiracy to commit murder. Damon's whole body shook with fear. He could not believe his luck.

"Drop your weapons and put your dick in the dirt! Now!"

Damon was in a state of shock. He thought that he had dropped his guns when he raised his hands to surrender.

"Drop your weapon!"

Shots rang out and hit his body from three different directions with each bullet doing more damage than the one that

came before it. The impact of the gunfire spun Damon around like a spinning top. He was later announced DOA when he arrived at Rivertown Hospital.

The authorities later reported that Damon shot first and then they returned fire. They also pinned all the recent slayings that were happening in the city on him. The sheriff's department held a press conference and stated that Damon was the possible mastermind and drug overlord of some local gangs that were terrorizing the city with a drug war. He-Man and Frankie returned back to the force, but shortly after, they were killed in a mysterious car crash. Slim reopened the Hole in the Wall and went on to rule his empire for the next thirty years.

THE END

"OK, thank you, Mr. Jarosinski. I'll be there within the hour." Damon ended the call and made his way down to coffee house.

As Damon drove, he knew there was a possibility that Handsome Vinnie could be trying to set him up. Damon had no other options, so he was forced to play with the cards that he was dealt. He pulled up two blocks from the coffee house and parked. He made the short walk so he could blend in as a patron. Damon walked into the noisy coffee house where the majority of people were Polish. He took a seat at a booth and looked over the menu. A few minutes later, a husky voiced waitress sat at his table with her pen and notepad.

"Good evening, sir. Today's special is a twelve-ounce cup of Zimbabwe coffee with your choice of a hot glazed donut or a chocolate iced cruller. If you turn the menu to the back, we have a few select deli sandwiches," the waitress advised as she smacked on her bubble gum.

"I'll just take water for now, and could you let Mr. Jarosinski know that I'm here to see him," Damon advised, catching her by surprise.

"Oh...oh. Are you Damon? Mr. Jarosinski has been expecting you. Go into the men's room. There is someone waiting for you in there." The waitress walked off hurriedly, heading to the kitchen.

Damon took a few moments before he headed to the restroom. When he entered the men's room two people were visible. Barney was sitting in a stall with his pants still up, and the other one, Albert, was scrubbing his hands thoroughly as if he was getting ready to perform open-heart surgery. Damon noticed the oddness of the men, but he still continued inside the restroom. He began to wash his hands in the sink when Barney

came from the stall and put a gun to his back. Albert stopped washing his hands and began to frisk Damon for weapons and wires as he dried his hands on his shirt.

"He's clean."

"All right then, follow us," Barney commanded.

Barney opened the stall where he had been sitting and opened the wall behind the toilet. He pushed Damon through as they walked inside. He then turned back around, closed the trap door, and sat back into position. Albert whispered in the ear of a better-kept gentleman. He was about six foot two, with salt and pepper wavy hair, slicked to the back. He wore a six-thousand-dollar blue and white pinstriped suit with a pair of midnight blue crocodile shoes that matched his eyes.

"Damon, let's get right to it. I had you checked out and there seems to be a hit on your head by Mr. Slim. So I will take your story as true. Now, quickly tell me your plan on how to get rid of our little problem because there is always someone watching," Handsome Vinnie said as he turned on the surveillance monitor, pointing at a white man dressed in a cheap business suit who sat impatiently at one of his tables.

"Shit, the police," Damon said.

"Yes, it is the fucking police. Don't turn chicken shit on me now."

"Well it's like this. I'm going to call Slim and tell him that I will give him back my share of the money if he would spare my life. I'm going to tell him to meet me at the old Kingsway department store, and that's when we'll take him out."

"What time is all this going down?" Vinnie asked.

"Well, it is four now, so I'll call him at eight and tell him to meet me at midnight."

"All right, me and the boys will go set up shop at six, but you better be there by nine. Do you understand?"

"Yes, Mr. Jarosinski, I'll be there."

"Good. Maybe after all this is over, you could come and work for me?"

"Thank you, Mr. Jarosinski, I would like that."

The two men shook hands and Albert led Damon back through the secret passageway. Just as Damon walked out of the restroom, the white man who they saw on the TV monitor was walking in. The man turned his head back to Damon, openly staring at him. Damon left the coffeehouse quickly before the man could come back from the restroom. Damon drove for about ten minutes before he dialed He-Man.

"Yeah," the voice on the other end answered in a low whisper.

"He-Man, we got to talk," Damon said urgently.

"I know. Where are you? I'll send someone to come pick you up," He-Man said suspiciously.

"No, I can't move around like that. Meet me at eleven thirty p.m. at the old Kingsway building."

"That place has been closed down for years. It would be too obvious," He-Man said, whispering.

"What would be too obvious? Look, dawg, that's where I'll be. Either you're there or you're not. Eleven thirty," Damon informed him again and disconnected the call, taking control.

The bait was in place. Now all that was left to do was to set the trap.

Damon made his call to Slim, and his men reassured Damon that Slim would be there. Damon arrived at Kingsway a little after nine. The side door to the old department store was

kicked in, so he knew someone was inside. Damon took the safety off the two-caliber gun and walked in cautiously.

"Hey, Mr. Jarosinski, it's me, Damon! Mr. Jarosinski?"

"Damon, come over here," Handsome Vinnie called as he shone a bright flashlight in Damon's face from the top of the stairs.

Damon joined Vinnie and about thirty of his crew as they set up ambushes throughout the abandoned department store.

"Damon, I want you to stick by me. If this turns out to be a trap for me, I'm going to make sure that you get a bullet in your head," Handsome Vinnie threatened.

Damon ignored him. He was too close to putting this all behind him to worry about his threats. The place was completely pitch black except for the speckles of sunlight that shined through the cracks and broken windows. Glass crumbled from under the footsteps of the new trespassers as they entered. The figures walked in slowly as their faces remained hidden in the shadows of the doorway.

"Damon the Damien, where the fuck are you?" He-Man called out.

"Who the fuck is that?" Handsome Vinnie whispered to Damon.

"That's He-Man and I think his partner, Frankie. They're police officers Slim has working for him. They're a bonus for trusting me. They are the same cops who followed you and bugged the hotel room that you were busted in," Damon said to Vinnie, hoping he hadn't overdone it.

"Oh really?" Handsome Vinnie smiled.

"But we got to get them quick because Slim will be here soon, and he's the bigger fish that we need to fry."

"Damon, come out here! We need to talk," Frankie commanded.

Handsome Vinnie gave the order in the earpieces of his men who were hidden closest to the entrance. Silencers muffled the sound of the assault riles as they poured into shadows that occupied the front door. The fire from the guns flickered and revealed the faces of He-Man and Frankie as they were chopped down.

"Drag their asses to the other fucking side and get back into position," Handsome Vinnie ordered.

"That was fucking fantastic, wasn't it, little homey?" Handsome Vinnie asked Damon as he looked at his men while they obeyed his orders.

Gunshots rang out and the men who were carrying the corpses became corpses themselves. A swarm of bullets flew through the closed-down department store, hitting a slew of targets as an army of killers entered. Handsome Vinnie called out from the top stairs for his men to return fire as he unloaded onto the lower level. Bodies from both groups were piling high. Damon knew it was time for him to make his exit. He'd been there a few hours earlier so he could map out some escape routes. As he headed to the back of the building, trying to escape through a street exit, Handsome Vinnie confronted him.

"Hey, where the fuck you think you going?" Vinnie asked with his machine gun blasting into the air like a rebel celebrating a victory.

"I'm not going anywhere. I'm looking for Slim. That muthafucka' ain't getting away alive!"

"Cut the bullshit. You think you fucking smarter than me? You think you can fucking outthink Vinnie Jarosinski? Tony,

gon' and bring Mr. Fuller his fucking bonus," Vinnie told one of his men as he smirked at Damon.

Damon thought about shooting Vinnie with the twin calibers and dashing for the back exit, but he wasn't sure where he had all his men positioned. He didn't want to come this far just to get killed.

"Here you go, Mr. Jarosinski," Tony said as he handed over Doobaby.

"Don't look so shocked, Mr. Fuller. You think you can get me to do your dirty work for you while you ride off into the sunset? No, I did some checking on you, my little friend. I know your real mama is dead and your flipped-out foster mom lives with her sister. You're a fucking orphan and the only friend you have is this fucking little prick that always seems to put your life in fucking danger." Vinnie stopped for a moment because gunshots were getting close to where they were standing. After some of his men flew past him, returning fire upon their attackers, he continued.

"Your fucking friend here just couldn't keep his mouth shut. He said you sent him on the bus to Ohio, except when the bus made a stop at Grand Rapids he got off and hopped on another bus back to Detroit. He also gave me info on those cops that worked for Slim. So He-Man and Frankie work for Slim, now?" Handsome Vinnie asked sarcastically.

"We found your homeboy hiding out at this bitch, Janice's, house. My little cousin Sal was banging that black bitch and little Doodoo over there kept calling. So my cousin Sal asked who the fuck is that calling you like they fucking crazy? She replied that it was this small-time, broke muthafucka named Doobaby that wouldn't stop bugging her after she gave him some pussy. Now remember, I already had all your information and we

were searching everywhere for this dumb prick. So my cousin called me up and told me that this fucker is calling the black bitch that he was boning. She called the little squirt over and the rest is history." Vinnie hurried with the story so they could get back into the gun battle.

"Doobaby, you stupid muthafucka, I told you to lay low for a while," Damon yelled.

"Oh, fuck you, man. I was starving on that bus, plus I got motion sickness."

"Motion sickness? I can't believe you could be so fucking dumb!"

"Nigga, I'm dumb? You the one who got us here in the first place."

"Well maybe if you never stole any money from He-Man, then we wouldn't fuckin' be here."

"Well, maybe if you hadn't begged me to sell drugs when I warned you about Black Sam, then…"

"Both of you shut the fuck up! Damon, go fucking bring Slim to me or Tony will put a bullet in your friend's head right now," Vinnie insisted as Tony held a gun to Doobaby's head.

"I don't give a fuck about him. Do it," Damon stated as bullets flew past Vinnie, barely missing him.

"Fuck it, kill them both!" Vinnie said as he shot back at the army that was slaughtering his men.

Doobaby made a run for it as Tony gave chase. Vinnie fired his rifle in Doobaby's direction as Tony ran after him. When Vinnie turned back around, the tip of Slim's blade greeted him as it dug into his belly. Slim made a sharp turn with the knife and Vinnie's intestines fell out onto the floor. Damon only had a few seconds to decide if he should try to escape or if he should try to rescue Doobaby. Slim withdrew his knife from Vinnie and

saw Damon watching from a few feet away. Slim called for his men to go after him. Now was the time for Damon to make his move.

If Damon should try to escape, go to the next page.
If Damon should try to rescue Doobaby, go to page 74.

A Meeting With the Devil

Damon had risked his life for Doobaby twice. Three was not going to be a charm. Damon dashed for the back exit like Kevin Garnett running under the hoop for a rebound. People were getting shot all around him as he ran. He made it to the exit, but someone must have bolted the door from the outside.

"So we finally meet," Slim said after he had backed Damon into a corner. "You are a very clever young man, trying to kill all your enemies with one sweep. Except no single man can kill me. You need a real army to take me. Just like Chrysler, GM, and Ford made this city the Motor City, I made it the Murder Capital. I don't give a fuck about life, but I rule it effortlessly. I send my men out like great locusts to attack and make this city and its citizens suffer. I allow them to kill women and children with no remorse. I condone drive-bys, regardless of the innocent bystanders who may get killed. My gangs push drugs from East Gratiot all the way to West Eight Mile Road. If my men are low on dough, then they are permitted to rob, beat, and even murder to make ends meet. I laugh at how much power I have over these dumb niggas who would kill each other over a pair of Cartier glasses. My people are ignorant, but I'm smarter than them, so I don't mind controlling them like puppets."

Damon's eyes darted around, looking for an out, but Slim had him completely boxed in. He had no choice but to stand there while Slim continued his speech.

"What other race do you know that doesn't own anything, but always has the best iced watch? We allow Arabs and Chinks to move into our ghettos and make millions while we struggle to feed our families and pay our bills. Drugs are the best thing that whitey did for us in the ghetto. So what if they make

our brothers into fuckin' walking zombies? At least some of us are now able to get a piece of the American pie because of these little white stones they call crack.

"Well, little homey, your time is up. You probably didn't know that was my establishment that you robbed, but no matter how old you are, you have to be made an example of. I would look soft if I let you live and get away with that type of shit. You know the code of the streets. Ignorant? Yes, but I've built my street career off it. After I put a hit on my first and only love Deborah Daniel Fuller, I lost all compassion and mercy for anyone. After a few years had passed, I found out that she had my son. I didn't search for the little nigga, though. Maybe he will find a better path in life than I did, but unfortunately for you, you will not," Slim finished as he revealed the twelve-inch butcher knife.

"Deborah Fuller? That was my mama! You killed her? You black son of a bitch!" Damon screamed as he pulled the two .44 caliber guns from under his shirt.

Slim stared at the young boy that he had felt a strange connection with. He had never talked to someone so much before he killed. He stared in the boy's face and realized that he did look familiar. Besides having his mother's eyes, Damon looked just like Slim with the same shaped face and big lips. They also shared their quickness to draw. But their family reunion was cut short by the nose ends of Damon's pistols that had locked in on Slim.

Damon was infuriated. His face turned red as he thought about the way his mother and uncles were gun downed. Damon knew that Slim had set them up. If it wasn't for his mother hiding him under the bed, he would have been killed as well. Sirens sounded outside the building as police began to raid the store. Every gang member stopped fighting and began to flee.

"Come on, Damon, put down the gun. We can talk about this later. You are my son," Slim said as he reached quickly behind his back and pulled out his glock, letting off three shots.

Damon unloaded with quick speed, hitting Slim six times in the chest before catching one in the shoulder. Damon staggered back as he tried to catch his balance. The police were everywhere; Damon realized that he had no choice but to surrender. Doobaby came out of nowhere and grabbed Damon by the waist to keep him from falling. Doobaby wiped Damon's prints off the two pistols with the side of his shirt, then dropped them by Slim's corspe. Damon showed Doobaby an exit that was just beyond the police's reach. They made it out of the employees' door and strolled out casually. A blue minivan that must have been left by one of Slim's men sat running about six feet away from the exit. Doobaby loaded Damon in and they sped off into the city.

"You OK?" Doobaby asked his friend.

"I'll live. How did you get away from Vinnie's man?"

"The dumb muthafucka was chasing me while trying to answer his cell phone and he tripped and shot himself." Doobaby laughed.

"I left you, Doobaby. You kept fucking up, man. I put my life on the line for you too many times."

"Did I do good this time? Doobaby asked.

"Yeah man, you did good this time. Thanks for saving me."

"Aww, don't start crying on me now. So what bank do you think we should rob real quick so we can get back on our feet?"

"There you go with that bullshit again!"

"Hey, we should at least go to He-Man's and see if we can find the money from the heist, though."

"Will you shut up and take me to the hospital, fool? I'm over here bleeding to death and you're talking nonsense."

"Damn, I won't say nothin' else."

"You know what? That is probably one of the smartest things that I've ever heard come out your mouth," Damon said as both men laughed.

THE END

Resolution

Even though Doobaby was the biggest retard Damon had ever known, he could not abandon him. Damon ran behind Tony as he chased Doobaby into the warehouse. Tony tried answering his cell as he ran and fired at Doobaby. When he got the flip part of his phone up, he tripped over a crate and shot himself in the face.

"Doobaby, you OK?" Damon asked while breathing heavily.

"Yeah...man. A little exhausted from all of this running, but I'm straight. Did you see that dumb muthafucka? He shot himself trying to answer his fucking phone." Doobaby laughed.

"Well...um...you're lucky he did," Damon advised.

Doobaby's smirk suddenly dropped from his face, and instead his expression revealed fright.

"What's wrong?" Damon asked as Doobaby pointed behind him.

"Slim!!!" Doobaby yelled as he ran toward Damon.

Slim raised his knife and stabbed Damon in the back of his neck. The first stab didn't penetrate that well, but the second and third ripped a hole through Damon's Adam's apple. Doobaby rushed forward and wrestled Slim to the ground, trying to take away his knife. They tussled back and forth over the blade. Sirens could be heard outside as the police raided the store.

Slim finally pinned Doobaby down by grabbing him by the throat with one hand as he tried to stab him with the knife in the other. Doobaby stuggled for air as he held back the knife from slicing his throat. One of Damon's guns had fallen from his hand when he hit the ground. Doobaby stretched his arm, trying to reach the weapon as Slim's blade kept getting closer and closer

to his neck. After several tries, Doobaby was finally able to retrieve it. He grabbed the pistol and unloaded the clip into's Slim's chest.

Slim's face was in shock. He could not believe that he had been shot. His mouth was wide open as blood poured from his lips. Slim staggered to his feet, dropping the bloody butcher knife. Doobaby scrambled up and tried to escape through the fire exit, but it was locked. Slim laughed at Doobaby as he tried his best to keep his balance. Doobaby looked down at his fallen friend and Slim laughed harder before spitting blood into Doobaby's face. Doobaby hit Slim upside his head with the pistol, causing Slim to fall backward. Doobaby bent over and began beating Slim over and over with the handle of the gun until he could no longer hear him breathing.

"Put the weapon down!" the officer yelled as his backup arrived.

Doobaby looked around and saw nothing but a tight circle of blue shirts with guns. He dropped his weapon and lay face down on the floor. What seemed like a hundred officers handcuffed him and dragged him out to a squad car. Doobaby sat in the back of the police vehicle watching as a dozen news vans and police cars pulled in and out. Families of some of the murdered, screamed and cried as police held them back from crossing the yellow tape. The screams and commotion were so loud that Doobaby couldn't even hear himself think.

A young police officer yanked open Doobaby's door and began to pound him with his flashlight.

"There are eight officers dead because of you muthafuckers! One was my partner!" the officer screamed as he kept whacking Doobaby.

Finally a couple of officers grabbed the cop out the car and settled him down. Another cop got into the car and sped off to the police station with the sirens blasting. Doobaby lay handcuffed in the backseat, battered and bruised. He laughed hysterically as he recalled the lie that Damon used to tell him.

"Doobaby, I promise I will not allow you to get me killed."

Doobaby closed his eyes and wept silently as he waited for fate to take him to his destiny.

THE END

People who live in Detroit are significantly more likely to kill each other than people who live in New York or Chicago.

In the 15-24 age group, 232 black men for every one hundred thousand can expect to be killed every year.

From 1972 to 2002, 94% of black victims were killed by blacks.

Nationally, homicide is the leading cause of death for black men ages 15-24.

Among males age 25 to 29, 12.6% of blacks were in prison or jail, compared to 3.6% of Hispanics and about 1.7% of whites.

The Department of Justice, Bureau of Justice Statistics has also show that based on current rates of first incarceration, an estimated 32% of black males will enter State or Federal prison during their lifetime, compared to 17% of Hispanic males and 5.9% of white males.

Sources:

http://www.ojp.usdoj.gov/bjs/

Harrison, Paige M., & Allen J. Beck, Bureau of Justice Statistics, Prison and Jail Inmates at Midyear 2004 (Washington, DC: US Dept. of Justice, April 2005), p. 11.

http://www.cdc.gov/men/lcod.htm#black

NOV. 2006

O-BORO BOOKS
PRESENTS

GHETTO HEAVEN

ERICK S. GRAY
(AUTHOR OF BOOTY CALL)

COMING SOON FROM

O-BORO
BOOKS

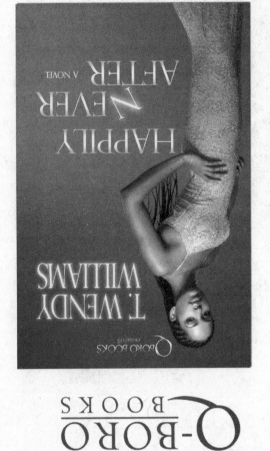

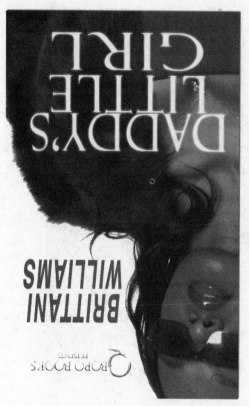

FEB. 2007

DADDY'S LITTLE GIRL

BRITTANI WILLIAMS

Q-BORO BOOKS
PRESENTS

COMING SOON FROM
Q-BORO
BOOKS

COMING SOON FROM

Q-BORO
BOOKS

PREVIEW
CHAOS IN THE CAPITAL CITY
By D. Mitchell

Coming soon from Q-Boro Books

Chapter Two
Operation Safe Streets

I walked defiantly down the small, one-way street named Quebec Place, strolling with a jay of marijuana in my hand. Under the cloudy skies which represented the mood on our side of the city most days, I made my way for the playground, hoping to run into the fellas and see what we were getting into.

The Raymond Recreation Center consisted of a large field, basketball and tennis courts, the rec building and a children's play area. Raymond Elementary School was just on the other side of a grassy hill. Most times the fellas and I lounged on the jungle gym in the children's play area. Other times we would huddle behind the rec and gamble.

Our little crew, known as the QBC mob, consisted of about twenty to twenty-five people at any given time, though it never seemed to stay steady for more than a couple of months. At some point or another everyone did a little time. Once in a while someone was retired by way of violence. DC was hectic like that. I'm sure many of the residents wondered how life in the nation's capital could be so tough.

I ventured up the playground and found Vil and Shorty doing exactly what I expected—laughing, joking, and smoking. We had little cliques within our crew that hung together a little tighter than others in the gang. Our clique consisted of Vil, Shorty, Slim, Jake, and me.

Vil was the senior member and accepted leader of our crew. Vil, who resembled me in physical appearance, was very streetwise and devious. Shorty was small and tough. He was like Joe Pesci's character on the movie *Goodfellas*, always hype and ready for whatever. Jake was born here in America, but his people were from Jamaica. He was even darker than me and talked with a slight accent. Jake had all types of connections in the world of illegal activity. Slim, nicknamed for his tall and slender frame, was the quiet killer of the bunch. They called me D, taken from the first letter in my name. I was the neutral one with book smarts who got caught up in the wrong crowd. I did some pretty mean things with my friends and basically did them because of my friends and poor judgment.

"What's up wit' you?" Vil greeted me.

"D," Shorty acknowledged.

"Fellas. I see y'all got a nice rotation goin' over here," I said.

"Yeah. It's goin' be nicer when you put your jay in it," Shorty responded.

"Oh, it ain't nothin' goin' on. This here is a head jay."

"Whatever. You better pass that shit," Vil said. I took about five long pulls and passed the jay to Shorty. Vil passed me the jay he had.

"Vil, you hollered at your man yet?" I asked.

"Who is that? My man with the cracks or my man with the weed?"

"The cracks."

"No doubt. I got an ounce up off him early this mornin'. What you need?" The jays rotated between us again.

"I need a quack," I said, using the slang for a quarter of an ounce.

"Oh naw, I don't got that," he said, snickering. "I can decent you up wit a ho-ho," slang for wholesale, "or I'll give you his number and you can page him your damn self."

"Are you goin' give me seventy joints for my two fifty?" Shorty and Vil looked at each other with astonishment. Then they looked at me.

"Stop playing' wit' me, son," Vil said with a slight grin on his face.

Shorty added his two cents. "You shouldn't even give his bitch-ass the number." I got up from the sitting position and walked over to Shorty.

"Don't come over here playin' and . . ." His words were interrupted by the body shot I delivered. He sighed. "You goin' make me go get my joint."

"I'll give you fifty-five for your two fifty," Vil said.

"It's a bet," I agreed.

DC was a unique city for many reasons. It was the capital of the world's most powerful country. It hosted the political, judicial, law enforcement and military infrastructure for the entire nation. The city was predominantly black. The crime rates per capita in DC were some of the highest for all cities nationwide. The most unique aspect about the city was that in spite of the heavy presence of the government, it was our show. Many laws were made in DC and most of them were broken in DC.

The White House and FBI Headquarters were less than three miles away and I, like most of my friends, had never been or wanted to visit either. Their proximity to our location meant absolutely nothing. On any given day we had plenty of crack, weed, heroin and boat (also known as PCP) to go. Handguns were explicitly illegal in the city unless you were an officer of some sort, yet almost all of us had at least one.

When crack was first introduced to DC, the bad aspects of the city quickly became ugly. Young black men began making thousands of dollars a week and some in a day, easily exceeding the salaries of professionals with advanced degrees. Gang-related violence increased tenfold and the murder rate skyrocketed. Guns became very accessible. The younger generation, which I was a member of when the epidemic hit, saw the fast life and that was all that many of us ever aspired to be a part of. The "I want to be a doctor or lawyer" stuff went out the door when crack came in. The money, the women, and other material things seduced most of us to try our hand in "the game."

"You in da club tonight, son?" Vil asked me.

"I don't know. I gotta get my money together first."

"I'll do that for you after we finish hitting these jays," he said, concerning the drug deal. I nodded.

After we finished the jays, we got up and headed for Vil's house. When we got to the corner of Tenth and Quebec, the roar of car engines caught us by surprise. Figuring that it may very well be the police, we prepared to make a hasty exit as Vil and Shorty began tossing contraband. Before we could start running good, two unmarked police cars sped down the street and came to a screeching halt right in front of us. We turned to see that two more squad cars and another detective's car sped up Tenth

Street and cut off our escape route. All twelve of the officers hopped out with their guns drawn. They forcefully hauled us over to one of the cars and began a thorough search.

"Damn, it smells like we just missed the party. Y'all done smoked all the weed up?" a white, plainclothes police officer asked. His question went unanswered. I noticed something very different about the officers. They all wore the cheap looking police jackets that usually had MPD for Metropolitan Police Department written on them, but their jackets were different.

"Well, since we can't take y'all in at this particular moment, I'll fill y'all in on what's goin' on," the white officer continued. "There's an initiative in effect called Operation Safe Streets." He turned so that we could read the yellow lettering on the back of his jacket. "To make it short and simple fellas, it's like the zero tolerance policy we ran last summer, except it isn't citywide. It only applies to triflin'-ass neighborhoods like this.

"We know that y'all have been puttin' in a lot of work on these streets the last couple of years, so some pretty important people decided to hook y'all up with some vacation time. It's our job to make sure y'all get there." The other officers laughed at their partner's jokes. My friends and I were not amused.

"From this point on, this is our neighborhood. We'll be here around the clock tryin' to get y'all up out of here. We're givin' this neighborhood the works. We're gonna set up roadblocks, sting operations, foot patrols, bikes—the works.

"If you get caught with a joint of marijuana, you're goin' to jail. You get caught drinkin'," he paused mid-sentence, "hell, I don't even think y'all are old enough. If y'all get caught with alcohol, you're goin' to jail. If we catch you with crack, you're not comin' back. If we catch you with a gun…"

"You might catch a hot one," one of the other officers chimed in. They thought that was funny too.

"Effective immediately," the white officer continued, "this is a 100 percent drug-free community. Anyone who violates that 100 percent is goin' away for a long time. This is our 'hood now, fellas. Y'all better give your boys the heads up, 'cause it's not gonna be pretty."

They all left as quickly as they came. After they were out of sight, my friends began to retrieve their drugs. We continued up the street.

"The only reason his white-ass told us all that is because he knew that we was gonna hip the fellas anyway," Shorty said.

"It's some bullshit. All they goin' do is harass us all the time and try slow down our money," Vil said.

"They just wanna show the media and politicians they're bein' tough on crime by comin' down and puttin' the press on us. They just put a name on it this time." We took his warning lightly.

Later that evening, the whole crew was up on the jungle gym. There were fifteen of us smoking large amounts of marijuana and drinking everything from forty-ounce beers to Remy and Hennessy VSOP. Everyone was high, drunk and ready to party.

The Go-Go, one of the rowdiest and raunchiest ghetto parties around, featured live bands doing improvisations of popular hip-hop songs and a few songs of their own. The show usually started about ten or eleven. We never entered before twelve.

Almost every gang or crew in the city did the same thing that we were doing before they entered the club. Just about everyone who entered was smacked. There were a lot different

'hoods from all over the city in a not-so-large room. Go-Go's caused a lot of fights and most of the altercations that led to one neighborhood beefing with another. A few of them have made national headlines.

We were just preparing to mount up when Shorty noticed two cars driving through the alley. "Who in the hell is that in the alley? Somebody 'bout to get punished," he said as he pulled a gun from his waistband.

Everyone stared down the vehicles trying to make out who they were. They drove slowly through the alley, just on the other side of the field.

"It might be them niggas from up Second Street," Shorty said. After he said that, about eight of us instantly pulled guns from our waistbands or pockets.

Finally the cars passed underneath a lamp in the alley and their identities were revealed.

"It's the Jumps!" Vil said as everyone scattered instantly. The unmarked police cars quickly accelerated over to the steps that led to the play area where we had stood a few seconds before. On the basketball court about thirty yards away from the play area we heard car doors slam, which meant they begun the foot pursuit and the drivers would try to cut us off with their cars. That's what usually happened, but they never saw me again that night. We took the police a little more seriously after that incident.

TIME OUT

FLIP BOOK NOW TO READ